MAGIC
GUN

Center Point
Large Print

Also by Max Brand® and available from
Center Point Large Print:

The Red Well
Daring Duval
Sour Creek Valley
Gunfighters in Hell
Red Hawk's Trail
Sun and Sand
The Double Rider
Sunset Wins
Jigger Bunts
Stagecoach
The Wolf and the Man
Out of the Wilderness

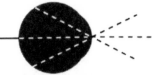

**This Large Print Book carries the
Seal of Approval of N.A.V.H.**

MAGIC GUN

A Western Duo

MAX BRAND®

CENTER POINT LARGE PRINT
THORNDIKE, MAINE

This Center Point Large Print edition
is published in the year 2019 by arrangement with
Golden West Literary Agency.

November 2019
First Edition

The name Max Brand® is a registered trademark with the
United States Patent and Trademark Office and cannot be
used for any purpose without express written permission.

Printed in the United States of America
on permanent paper.
Set in 16-point Times New Roman type.

ISBN: 978-1-64358-405-8

The Library of Congress has cataloged this record
under Library of Congress Control Number: 2019946827

MAGIC
GUN

The Danger Lover

I

That stage of woodcraft when the nose is burned at the tip, the cheeks at the cheek bone, the neck in a fiery rim where the top of the coat-collar touches, and the wrists are banded with a painful crimson, had been reached by Hugh Collier. But Collier was an optimist and did not object to these unpleasantnesses. He had gone into the mountains to find health, and he remembered a maxim out of his school reader which declared that the nut with the sweetest kernel is sure to possess the hardest shell. So, equipping himself with a horse, a small pack of food and other essentials, a rifle, a Colt revolver, and a fishing rod, he had pushed off into the wilderness alone; not because of a surplus of courage or knowledge of the wild, but because he could not afford a guide. Besides, somewhere he had read of the man who made his journeys through mountain and desert with only his rifle and a pouch filled with salt. Hugh Collier decided that if he had in addition to the rifle and salt, a horse, a fishing rod, a pack of provisions, a revolver, and other odds and ends, he certainly should be able to live in the wilderness. For he had a logical mind, and like most logicians he sometimes missed the important premise, no matter how true his conclusions might be.

For ten days, now, he had voyaged through the mountains. He found the nights bitterly cold, icy fingers of wind continually thrusting down his back or gripping his feet. He found the days scorching hot outside the shelter of the trees. He had fished in twenty streams and caught nothing but a pair of suckers, loaded with bones. He had shot at fifty squirrels, rabbits, chipmunks, and even had had a chance at a deer. But he had not added one morsel of fresh meat to his diet! However, he retained his high spirits.

On the second morning, his horse had proved a bit kinky in the fresh of the day and had bucked off Hugh Collier five times in a row.

"Practice," said Collier, "makes the master." And on the sixth attempt he managed to stay in the saddle.

And on every succeeding morning he had been pitched headlong. He had collected a dozen bruises from these falls, but they had taught him two things—a little of the art of staying a longer time in the saddle, and also how to relax in every muscle when heaved into the air, so that he would not strike the ground a tense, muscle-hardened unit. And, finally, on this tenth morning perhaps the horse had not bucked so hard, or his newly acquired skill stood him in some stead, but after the pitching ended, he was gratefully and somewhat dizzily aware that he was still in the saddle.

This, because he was a very simple fellow whose heart could be filled by small victories, made Hugh Collier rejoice, and he entered upon the day convinced that he would do better in everything. In fact, he had landed one bite and one sucker that day at fishing. He had shot so close to a rabbit that the flying jack had spy-hopped from the kicked-up dust. And now in the afternoon he found himself on a hill overlooking a little town—the first sign of human habitation since he entered the wilderness—conscious of a ravenous appetite, a clear eye, and a sense of joyous being that welled upward and upward like sparkling water from a spring.

He sat for a time, one hand on his hip, his chest out, with the air of some armored conquistador gazing down on a rich Indian city. For he was a discoverer, in fact. He did not know the name of this town, he hardly guessed what state it stood in, he had not followed map or chart along the trails that he pursued. Indeed, he merely had gone headlong where his fancy took him, and that was deeper and deeper into the loftier sea of mountains.

He was so delighted with himself that every feature of the landscape was individually pleasant to him. With the eye of an artist he drew for memory the thin silver twists of wood smoke above the chimneys of the town, the whirlpool of dust rising from the street, and the shapes of the shacks, some of them mere cracker boxes, some with little front verandahs which gave them the look of visored caps thrown down on the ground. It was as plain, as cheap, as ordinary, as perishable, as ramshackle, as ugly, as haphazard a village as ever appeared even in the West, where man mars the natural beauty of the country. But to young Hugh Collier it seemed a charming place. For one thing, it was as different as possible from the town in which he sat perched on the top of a stool in a small bank, laboring late, praying that long hours and patient care would make up for a lack of business genius.

From this low crest a dim cattle trail wandered up the face of the hill, with all the perversity of a cow's ways visible upon its face. Sometimes it sagged to the side in broad loops where the declivity was most gentle, and sometimes it mounted the steepest angle in a straight upward line. But even this amused Hugh Collier. There was nothing on the whole face of Nature of which he disapproved, even the polished cliffs and the formidable cold snows of the mountains that lifted above the timber line all around him, nor the darkness of the forests that clothed their lower slopes in grand shadow. There was nothing in the whole animal kingdom that he did not love, even the gophers that burrowed holes into the ground for horses to step in and crack their shanks. The whole human species seemed to him filled with wisdom, genial kindness, and a heaven-given light!

But these things were true only as he looked West. Behind him lay a mirage of ugliness that floated into his thoughts unless he kept them occupied. He would not let the wide flat plains dawn on his memory again, or the paved streets of the towns, or the stiff houses which stood with dead faces side-by-side while the rain fell or the sun warmed them in vain, or the deadly quiet of the bank where business proceeded through the mortuary hush, with only the moan of the electric fan alternating on two sad notes through the endless afternoons.

This lay behind him. His back was turned toward it. He stretched out the arms of his spirit to this wild, rough fairyland. And all he needed to make his joy more complete, to make his ecstasy more perfect, was a shadow and seasoning of sorrow when he knew that before long he would have to stop his march and turn wearily back toward his duty, and the eight-hour day, the six-day week, the twelve-month year, the naked life. When he looked down at the distorted shadow of himself and his horse on the ground, he felt that his old life had been like that, a caricature and savage cartoon of the beautiful truth that life may be.

He was about to take that inviting downward trail when he heard the clinking of iron against rocks and, looking around, he saw a horseman riding along the ridge toward him on a very tired horse that stumbled, and jerked up its head, and stumbled again.

The rider sat straight and easy in the saddle, with one powerful hand controlling the movements of the failing horse, at the same time looking off across the hollow in which the village stood. When he came close to Collier, he called out with an abrupt sternness: "What town is that?"

"I don't know," said Collier.

"You don't know?" exclaimed the stranger, seemingly offended by this reply.

He rode straight up to Collier and brought his horse very near, as a few men have the habit of approaching unpleasantly near to those with whom they converse, as though they wish to lend an emphasis to voice or eye by their mere physical presence.

Collier drew a little on the reins. If he had been on foot he would have shrunk back somewhat.

"I'm a stranger here, too," he said.

"You're a stranger, are you?" said the other, keeping his eyes so firmly fixed on Collier's face that he seemed to be reading his heart's secrets. "You don't even know the name of that town?"

"No," Collier said as mildly as before.

But he returned the stare with a quiet observance. He was a timid man to whom a meeting

14

with a stranger was like a splash of cold water in the face, but he was not a coward.

"Nor the trail to Millerton?"

"No," said Collier.

The other flushed with impatient anger, and as he did so, Collier grew more interested than ever, because he saw a thin white scar that extended from his forehead, over his left eye, and straight down his cheek. It was hardly a defacement. It was little more than a thin white thread, but it stood out clearly as he flushed, and it was doubly interesting to Collier since he himself carried a very similar mark. It was not so distinct, with him, and it was not so perfectly regular, but when he himself blushed it could be seen. He had gotten it while climbing through a barbed-wire fence, pursued by the angry owner of a watermelon patch, many a year before. This similarity of scars gave him an odd feeling of kinship with the stranger, and made it easy for him to forgive the distinctly abrupt manner of the other.

"Millerton! Millerton!" the stranger repeated fiercely. "I'll never get there in time with this horse."

A touch of appeal came into his voice, asking Collier to bear witness to his hard luck.

"Hard as nails when he's working, tough as a nut, but soft from lazing around while I broke ground, and now look at him! Done up by fifty miles."

"Fifty miles?" Collier said, with every bone aching at the thought of such a ride. "Over this country it sounds like a lot."

"Why, he was a bird . . . he winged across the grades!" declared his companion. "Now he's done up, and I'm stuck! They'll file on my claim. . . ."

He gritted his teeth, and looked forward as though his will were struggling to transport him suddenly over the many tall ridges of the hills.

"Hello," Collier said warmly. "Somebody trying to jump a claim?"

"And they'll do it," said the stranger, "when a fresh horse would get me . . . Look here. I'll trade you horses, partner. Look this one over! Fagged now, but, otherwise, he's all that he looks. I'll take your bronco and ask no boot. Is it a go?"

He flashed out of the saddle as he spoke, and Collier blinked at such suddenness. He remembered many a tale he had heard of cheating in horse trades, but he could not fail to understand that there was a real pressure of emotion in his companion that seemed above and beyond any possibility of shamming.

"No boot, mind you. I'll take your horse the way he stands!"

He stripped off his own saddle and turned furiously on Collier.

"What's the matter? You want cash besides a horse like this?"

Collier was no expert judge of horses, but

even he could appreciate the long rein, the substance, the fine conformation of this tall bay. His forehead was broadly blazed, and there was a long white stocking up the near foreleg. A line from the old adage rang through his brain.

One white stocking, buy him. . . .

He slid down to the ground. "All right," he said, "it's a go!"

II

The lips of the stranger compressed a little, whether with regret that the trade had to be made, with sorrow at leaving his horse, or was it suppressed triumph struggling to form a smile?

At any rate, the saddles soon were changed, and the stranger flashed onto the back of Collier's former mount.

"You're the right sort," he said to Collier, holding out his hand, from which he had stripped the glove. "You don't take half a day to make up your mind."

His grip was like a contraction of strong iron hands under which Collier winced.

"Good luck to you!" said the other, and, touching the mustang with his spurs, he plunged down the slope. The dark pines closed about him, for an instant a noise of crackling brush sounded, and then Collier was alone with himself again, looking about in wonder at the suddenness of this change. As a squall to a sailor, so had this stroke of weather been to him.

Vaguely he noted, well to the north, a stream of half a dozen riders pouring over the brim of a hill and disappearing in the hollow beyond. Then he looked to his prize.

The gelding was thoroughly done up, as its rider had admitted, but it was a beauty, and someone has said that beauty in horses is not like beauty in women. It tells no lies.

Collier had too much heart to put his weight on that tired back, remembering how the bay had reeled under the tug of the tightening cinches. The village was close, it was sure to have harborage in it, and suddenly he yearned for a meal served on a table by hired hands. So he walked down the slope, leading his new horse carefully behind him.

A freckled boy, shirtless, hatless, sun-blackened, clad in just a baggy pair of what must have been his father's trousers, encountered him at the beginning of the dusty town street and cupped hands to hoot.

"Hey, are you scared to get on?"

But Collier waved a hand and smiled with disarming good nature. Nevertheless, the boy followed along with him, half mischievous, half curious, babbling questions and making personal remarks which proved that he trusted to a fleet foot and familiar ground.

"Where's the best hotel?" asked Collier.

"There ain't a best," said the boy. "There's only one, and nobody thinks that's good except Sam Hooley, and he's blind and ain't got teeth enough to eat meat no more. There's the hotel. That thing that looks like three barns kicked together and never straightened out none."

Its ugliness merely amused Collier, for it would have taken a great deal to damp his spirits on this day. The bay horse, for one thing, had recovered a good deal even on the walk down the hill and now pricked its ears forward a little as it entered a place where the smell of hay came to it. In the horse shed behind the barn, Collier put the gelding up and carefully rubbed him down with wisps of hay, then stood by for a minute and smiled with pleasure when he saw him begin to eat with a good appetite; for he knew that a hungry horse cannot be sick.

After that, he went in to take care of his own appetite.

The dining room was empty, but a sound of voices led him to the kitchen, where he found the waitress seated on the table with her knees in her arms while she chatted with the cook. Excessive fat had brought in that range rider

19

from the saddle to the kitchen, and he supported his excessive girth, now, with a broad sash girded around his hips. But still his stomach overflowed the measure. He looked at the stranger with a discouraging frown and pointed out that Collier had fallen between two stools, for he was late for dinner and early for supper.

"Well," Collier said humbly, "I don't want anything extra. Ham and eggs would do for me."

The cook turned to the waitress. "Ham and eggs would do for him," he said.

The waitress grinned. "The sun's got him," she said. "How many chickens had you heard talk since you arrived?"

"Ham and coffee and bread, I don't care what," Collier said.

"He's hungry," said the waitress. "Go on and feed him, Jack."

Jack grunted, but with a vicious side-glance at the stranger he admitted that: "Something would be coming up pretty soon."

Collier went back into the dining room, where he sat down at peace with himself.

The heat of the afternoon had ended. Through the window he saw the shadows sloping far and cool, with the promise of sunset not far away, and the breeze that touched his face was a soft mercy. The world was unflawed, beautiful, and good. If it contained some raucous voices and harsh faces, still the soul of the world was the soul of kindness. In the kitchen though he heard the cook complaining loudly, yet he also heard the frying pan at work.

A steaming platter was brought to him at last—a great, thin slab of ham, some warmed-over pone, a lukewarm dish of fried potatoes, and a huge earthen mug of coffee.

The waitress sat down on the table that faced him—chairs did not seem to interest her—and swung her heels while she watched Collier eat.

He found the ham almost hard enough to turn the iron points of the fork, and the girl grinned as she watched him.

"It ain't tough, is it?" she asked.

"A little bit," he admitted, looking up hopefully.

Her grin merely broadened. "It'll last longer, then," she observed. "Dad, he used to always say that tough meat made a good lawyer . . . I mean, it gives a man a lot of jaw. Try the pone. I made that myself."

"It's very good," Collier said untruthfully.

"If it was good," she replied, "there wouldn't be that much left from noon. I'm only learning, and if you learn on mistakes, I'm sure gonna graduate pretty high up. How long you been loose, partner?"

"Loose?" Collier said vaguely.

"Yeah. I mean . . . out of the corral, beyond the fence, unhobbled, through the gate, if you can

21

understand that any better. When was the bars left down?"

"You mean, when did I leave home?" Collier asked.

"You follow me perfect," she said. "You'd make a lead horse and a jerk-line leader, old-timer."

"I'm out vacationing," Collier announced, with a smile that invited a sharing in his joy.

"Hey!" yelled the cook from the kitchen door, as he slammed it open. "Are you gonna peel them potatoes?"

She regarded the just anger of the cook without dismay.

"He's out vacationing," she said to the kitchen man.

"You ain't, though," he replied hotly. "Because he's lost, ain't no reason that you gotta lose the way home."

"I'm not lost," Collier stated brightly.

"He ain't lost!" groaned the cook heavily.

"He's not lost, he says," repeated the waitress.

It was very odd, their way of echoing his words, as though they were passing an order down a line.

"As a matter of fact," Collier said, "I could hardly be lost, because, you see, I'm not going anywhere."

"He's not going anywhere!" exclaimed the cook.

"He's not . . . going anywhere," said the

22

waitress. "You better come and sit down, Jack. This is likely to keep on for a long time."

"What is?" asked Collier. "If I may ask," he added pleasantly, for he never forgot his manners. Good manners, said his book of maxims, may not be bread and butter, but they often lead the way to it.

"May he ask?" said the waitress.

"He may," said the cook. "Dog-gone me if I ain't beat!"

"By what?" Collier asked.

"The heat!" shouted the cook, his face convulsed.

And he retired into the kitchen, from which a curious booming sound presently issued.

"Is he ill?" Collier asked.

"He's only laughin' a little," said the girl, "and when he laughs it hurts his stummick, and that means he hurts all over. He hates to laugh. I seen him once pretty near choke to keep from laughin', and when Willie Hampton comes around, Jack starts heavin' things. You'd like to die, to hear Willie, the way he talks. I'm glad you ain't lost, though."

"Thank you," said Collier. "I'm just out . . . vacationing . . . wandering about, I hardly care where. You know what I mean."

"I'm tryin' to," she declared. "But it don't come too easy. What's your name?"

"Collier."

Her blunt manner was odd, but since he had done nothing to offend her, he smiled on her with perfect good fellowship. It was such a boyish, direct, and open smile. Moreover, he was so good-looking in spite of sunburned nose and cheeks, that the girl's lips twitched. She smiled in turn. Then she broke into hearty laughter.

"I suppose you're laughing at me?" Collier said.

"Me? At you? Of course I ain't. Why should I laugh at you?"

"I've been trying to think," he said.

"I couldn't laugh," she declared, "at a gent with a horse like the one that you brought in. Even if you wasn't in the saddle."

"He was very tired," Collier explained in a voice gentle with sympathy.

"Yeah?" she demanded harshly. "So you got down and walked?"

"He'd done fifty miles, you see."

"Fifty miles from where?" she asked, with a doubtful smile.

"From the north," he answered.

"Fifty miles from . . . say, young fellow, that would be through the mountains, if you follow me!"

"Of course I do," he said. "You can understand why he's tired."

"Fifty miles! That's a horse!" she announced. "Or else you add wrong. Where'd you get him?"

24

At this, it occurred suddenly to Collier that he had nothing to show in order to prove his ownership of that horse except the saddle which he had strapped upon its back. No doubt that was the explanation of the willingness of the stranger to trade. It would explain, also, the men who he had seen stream over the hill in the distance.

And Collier flushed gradually, and completely, and looked down at his coffee.

At last he glanced up, in order to make an answer, but as he did so, he heard a pair of quick thuds on the floor, and perceived that the noise was made by the descending heels of the girl.

She looked down at his flushed face with a species of frozen horror, and in another moment she withdrew—actually walking backward for a few steps, and then, whirling, she bolted for the kitchen door!

III

Hugh Collier glanced back in amazement, at this behavior, but decided it must be because of something left untended or undone in the kitchen. This reflection comforted him, but still he shook his head a little. So young, he thought, so pretty, and so rattlepated.

He heard from the kitchen a sudden bellow from Jack, then silence out of which grew swiftly

25

murmuring voices that sounded like the noise of running water.

He finished the difficult ham with a sigh, and started to polish off the cornpone next, in spite of its wooden density. He almost had finished when he heard the kitchen door creak again, then a brief whispering, and finally across the floor toward him other creakings progressed and brought before him Jack, with the waitress in the offing.

Some sort of reproof was apparently about to descend upon Collier, perhaps a demand for double price because of the inconvenience of the hour? He decided that he would pay at once, no matter what. Anything was better than trouble.

This decision he reached the more readily because he saw that Jack was actually white to the lips, which trembled with emotion, and so did his puffy cheeks.

"I was only wantin' to say, sir," Jack said, in a half stifled voice, "I was only wantin' to say, Mister . . ."

"Collier," the girl said in a stage whisper.

"Only wantin' to say, Mister . . . er . . . Collier," went on Jack, choking a little over the name, "that neither of us figured on who you would be. . . ."

"Not expectin' you for a long time yet," put in the waitress.

"Not for a week," Jack said, passing the tip of his tongue over purple-gray lips.

"And the way you come in so dead quiet . . . it set us on the wrong trail," added the waitress.

"Hopin' you won't hold it ag'in' us," said Jack.

"Because we're with you," declared the girl. "Right to the limit we're with you . . . and . . . and the rest of the boys."

"I might of knowed," went on Jack, who was breaking into a profuse perspiration, "I might've reckoned that quiet water is in the deepest pools. But I figured on somebody older."

"Ten year, I guess," the girl clarified, "and bigger, too."

Hugh Collier looked from one to the other with the blankest of eyes, and this vacancy in his regard appeared to bring them both closer to the verge of desperation.

Jack hastily ran a finger over his forehead. "Regardin' that dog-goned ham," he said, "which I reckon I got the wrong kind out, anyway, I gotta slab of venison back there that'd turn into steaks that'd melt in your mouth."

"I'll start up the fire right pronto, Mister Gadsden," said the waitress.

And her voice, which had been so pert and chipper before now, actually trembled with apprehension.

"But I'm not Mister Gadsden, whoever he may be," Hugh Collier corrected.

He flushed at the mistake that had been made, though apparently it had been much to his honor, and as he blushed he saw the eyes of both man and girl fasten upon him as though hypnotized with interest and with dread. It was not into his eyes that they looked, as people generally do when they are excited, but a little below and to the side, very much as though they dreaded to meet his full gaze.

Jack swallowed hard. His shirt collar was open; nevertheless, he loosened it still further as he gasped.

"You ain't Bill Gadsden, sure you ain't! I dunno whatever put such an idea into our heads," said Jack wretchedly.

But still he stared, like a dog guilty of a crime, and waiting for the heavy hand of the master.

"I'm a fool," the waitress put in. "I might of knowed . . . but then, I reckon that nobody heard. It'll stay sunk with us. Jack, you go and rush up them steaks, if you could hurry a mite, while I clean off the table . . . supposin' you'd eat a bite more, Mister . . . er . . ."

"Collier," Hugh stated.

"Sure . . . Mister Collier. If you got any appetite left, I mean to say."

"I'm still as hungry as a wolf," admitted Collier. "But I wouldn't like to trouble you here in the middle of the day when it's neither dinner nor supper, as you pointed out before, Jack."

Jack grew very white and gripped the back of a chair for support.

"That was a little joke, only. No harm meant. Have the steaks comin' up in a minute. Rush 'em right along."

He hurried toward the kitchen door with a tottering step, and the girl with deft and anxious hands proceeded to clear away the empty dishes from the table. Then, from a cupboard, she produced a rough cotton cloth, laundered white, which she shook out and spread with careful pats in front of Collier. Swiftly she fled here and there, but like a true woman of the woods her footfall made little noise, now that she was earnestly bent on business. She produced an empty sugar bowl filled with water and fragrant yellow wildflowers to decorate the board for Collier. She laid out a special service of cutlery, and stood back an instant, panting a little, and wistfully smiling to gain his approval.

"It's very fine," Collier said. "But this is a lot of trouble for you. You shouldn't be bothered. . . ."

She raised a hand in almost desperate protest. "If I'd taken a good look at the horse when it came in with you . . . but I didn't think none. And . . . if there's any word that you want passed around to the boys . . ."

She waited expectantly, but Collier, totally bewildered, shook his head.

"I'm afraid you still think I'm Gadsden," he said.

She laughed a little, her eyes wrinkling at him with a deep and friendly understanding. "I don't think nothin' except what I'm supposed to think," she said. "You trust Molly Peters for that, will you?"

And with this, she winked, and departed for the kitchen, smiling over her shoulder.

She left Collier still bewildered, but it was a pleasant confusion that surrounded him with such continued courtesy. He tried to understand, but since there was no clue, except that he was taken for one Bill Gadsden, apparently a man of fame and standing, and since he could not convince the good people that he actually was not that person, he decided that he would accept what the fortune of the day brought to him and then ride off on the morrow as fast as he could, trusting that the deceived hosts would not discover their mistake in the interim. It struck Collier as a delightful adventure, but presently he began to fall into an idle daydream, conjuring up the reality of the true Bill Gadsden. Doubtless a man who looked somewhat like him, but of course bigger, stronger of heart and hand, a man with fire in his eye and power in his brain!

Collier sighed a little.

He would have liked to be such a man himself. One who appeared even to the strong-handed mountaineers as a sort of hereditary prince, to be looked up to, and obeyed. What feats of courage and of skill had the true Bill Gadsden performed? What half-maddened broncos had he ridden with a secure seat? What lives of man and beast had he taken? What leadership had been his when he stalked through his young life, if already men looked upon him with such awful admiration?

Bill Gadsden! The very name had a raw, powerful sound in the ear of Collier, and he sighed again. Such a king among men he, at least, never could be.

In the meantime, the dining room was no longer empty.

At first he was aware of men who loitered past the windows, and then across the door that opened upon the front verandah. Always they were pausing at these apertures, and looking in upon the sole diner with keen glances. At last, two of them came sauntering into the room itself.

They were encountered by Molly Peters, who carried on a brisk conversation with them, in a subdued voice, but their gruff rejoinders eventually seemed to appease her. She allowed them to sit down at a distant corner table and served them coffee.

Then, flitting back to Collier, she hooked a thumb over her shoulder toward the newcomers.

"Is it all right?" she asked him breathlessly. "They're inside, y'understand?"

"Of course they are," Collier said. "And certainly it's all right. I don't want to run your hotel, Molly."

She favored him with the sweetest of smiles, as though he had made some giant concession, but immediately afterward, Jack bawled for her from the kitchen and she fled, to return with two huge, steaming venison steaks, brown, cross-marked by the black lines of the broiler. Canned vegetables flanked these steaks, and potatoes done into fancy shapes, and more coffee and thick cream, and hot biscuits which, when opened, sent up small geysers of steam.

It was a feast the mere contemplation of which made Collier loosen his belt. But then he fell to with gusto.

Other men had come in to watch his dinner. He was not surprised that they were curious at the sight of anyone eating in such quantity, but he was amazed by the smiles and the quick, covert salutes which he received when he looked around him, sometimes in the form of nods, sometimes brief waves of the hand. And always the eyes of the mountaineers shone when he glanced at them, as though his look kindled fire in their minds.

It was for the great Gadsden. It was all for him—this respect, this subtle and delightful homage. Hugh, for the moment a king of men with only a scepter of shadows, lifted his head and cast his regard slowly about the room. He allowed himself to acknowledge these salutations with brief gestures, and with nods in return. He permitted himself to smile a little.

And then he turned his attention back to his meal, amazed at himself, half ashamed and half enchanted by the position in which he found Hugh Collier placed. The president of the bank in which he worked was surrounded by the fear and the respect of the town in which he lived, but what was that to being surrounded by these brown-faced, wide-shouldered clansmen who looked ready to ride thunderbolts, or wrestle with them.

Lucky Bill Gadsden, happy Bill Gadsden, luckier and happier than any man Collier had conceived of before this day!

Someone sprang hastily through the doorway, looked wildly around him, and then came with a rush for Collier—a lean, quick-footed, fierce-eyed man.

He bent and muttered: "They're coming! Sheriff Lassiter, and nine men with him. They're comin' fast!"

Collier looked vaguely up to the messenger.

"I mean," repeated the other, frantic with a nervous fear: "They're here in town, now! They're headin' straight for the hotel. Some skunk has give them news, but you still got time to run for it! They's a fresh horse saddled . . . out through that window."

Suddenly, Collier put back his head and laughed.

"But," he said loudly, "let the sheriff come! I'll be glad to see him!"

IV

He had spoken with sufficient clarity to enable everyone in the room to overhear him, and they were all struck dumb by his words. The messenger recoiled violently. Another man leaped to his feet, his chair screeching loudly across the floor. Another sagged forward in his seat and stared at Collier with haunted eyes. While the little waitress pressed both hands against her face, gazing enchanted at her client.

As Hugh smiled about him at the effect of his last speech, he could not help contrasting this moment with all the greatest ones of his previous life, and what had they been, all of them rolled together, to be worthy of weighing against this brief second when he held many men, strong men, mute with what they considered his vast daring, his consummate surety?

He laughed again, glorying in that foolish instant of supremacy.

Ah, it was well enough to enjoy this single second of triumph and the few that might follow it, for the time would not be long before they learned that, in fact, he was an impostor who had been placed not even by his own volition in the shoes of another and a greater man. Why should he not be careless and self-assured when he knew that there was no danger? Let the law grip him with ever so strong a hand, he had in his innocence a power that would make the grasp of the law powerless.

The messenger lurched forward at Hugh again.

"Listen, chief," he said, "heaven knows I ain't tellin' you what to do. You know your business. Only . . . you heard what I said? It ain't no common runt . . . it's Lassiter himself that's comin' here. It's Lassiter!"

He spoke the word with awe and with dread, but Hugh Collier shook his head, and the waitress broke in, stammering a little: "It ain't any good, Bud. They's gonna be a . . . they's gonna be a showdown between 'em! Lassiter's hounded him too long. But, oh . . ."

Her voice trembled away to silence, and the messenger, after a last desperate look around him, groaned aloud and fled swiftly through the kitchen door.

There was a loud shout from that quarter, a scuffling, a tremendous clattering of pans. Then both entrances to the room were blocked. On the verandah stood a slender man, with a close-cropped black mustache which gave him

35

a distinctly foreign air—a dapper-looking, self-possessed fellow.

And that was Lassiter. Hugh felt that he could have told him at a distance of a thousand yards, so much did he stand out from his posse men, who were crowding around him as he came through into the dining room, with a naked revolver in his hand.

And in the kitchen doorway, at the same instant, appeared the messenger, Bud, gripped on either shoulder by armed men who had taken the hotel from the rear in time to prevent his escape. He walked sullenly in, his head high, and his bright eyes expectantly fixed upon Collier.

So were all other eyes fixed. Those of the posse regarding him with a suspicious keenness, prepared for any sudden and desperate move, and those of the mountaineers in a sort of savage readiness to fight for him, if he only would lead the way, or make a single gesture of defiance.

Hugh knew as much, instinctively, no matter how unfamiliar he might be with violence in any form. The mere lifting of his finger would plunge that room into battle, even to the crouching figure of the girl in the corner, fascinated with white-faced terror.

Upon these things, Hugh Collier looked mournfully, and yet with interest. What would the real Gadsden have done? How tiger-like and swift would have been his response, and while the mountaineers who seemed to adhere to him fought off the rest, how he would close on Sheriff Lassiter and fight out the battle to the end?

It seemed to Collier that he could see the battle, hear the shouts, smell the pungent sting of the powder smoke drenching the air.

He sighed and blinked as he saw Lassiter now standing just before him, with a revolver leveled at his breast, while he called out to his posse men to keep the others in the room thoroughly covered.

In a wide semicircle they formed, rifles at the ready, the muzzles pointing toward the mountain men, their backs turned upon the sheriff and his special prisoner. And Lassiter, laying his left hand on the edge of the table, slowly approached the mouth of his gun to the breast of Collier.

"I've given you your chance to make a play, Gadsden," he said. "I've given you every opportunity. You had from the time I left the doorway until this instant, but your nerve crumpled, did it? You couldn't stand the pinch of quite such a moment as this?"

Collier's hands were on the edge of the table. He folded them, now, and he smiled curiously back into the face of Lassiter.

Dreadful indeed it would have been to have this man as an actual enemy, and see the slight contraction of the lips, and the twitching of the fierce smile, from time to time, at the corners of the mouth. But all this concentrated and cold ferocity was meant for Gadsden, and not for him, and still Collier could smile, securely.

"Sit down," he invited.

"I ought to have you stick your hands up," said the sheriff. "I ought to slap irons on your wrists, Gadsden. But I won't. Listen to me!"

His voice purred like the snarl of an angry cat.

"There's still a chance for you if you want to take it. You see? I'm lowering my gun . . . putting it out of sight . . . I invite you, man to man, to fill your hand and have this out with me, Gadsden!"

His voice shook a little and so did all his body. But Collier knew that it was not fear, but only the excess of concentrated nerve power. So shakes the dynamo, whirring at full speed and generating a great current. So with fierce desire to kill, with will to battle, with intense hunger for the combat, Lassiter leaned a little toward Collier and glared at him.

The very color of the man's eyes changed, and grew—as Collier thought—yellow-tinted, brilliant as the eyes of a cat in the dusk of a corridor.

Yet still Collier, his hands folded, could smile, for no matter how near the peril seemed to him, he knew that it was in reality far away.

This silence of his, this steady smile, caused presently a curious change in the sheriff. For his glance lost part of its concentrated fury. His eye widened somewhat, and his lips twitched uneasily.

The gun that he had removed a little, inviting a hostile move on the part of the other, he now replaced upon the edge of the table, with the big muzzle turned directly upon the heart of Collier.

"You've been slippery and smooth, my friend," said Lassiter. "By heaven, when I think of all the times I've seen you against the skyline, and then winging out of sight, or gliding across an open doorway, or melting into a cloud of dust . . . It doesn't seem possible that I'm here with you, again, and that I'm holding you at the point of a gun. Twenty times I've cornered you before this, Gadsden, and twenty times you've slipped away. But I've never had you as close and sure as this. Tell me, man . . . tell me what makes you able to smile, still? Is there still some hope in your mind that you can get away from me again?"

"Do you think," Collier replied, the smile growing a little, "that I would have sat here all this time if I hadn't known that I could get out of your hands the moment I chose?"

"Get out of my hands? The moment you chose?" Lassiter leaned back ever so little in his chair. "Go on, man, go on! I'm listening. Perhaps you're to talk your way out?"

"Exactly that," replied Collier.

The sheriff laughed, with no trace of mirth in the sound.

"Oh, Gadsden," he said, "it's been a long trail that's brought me to you, but in spite of your confounded smiling . . . which is only assumed to impress these hunting dogs of yours around the room . . . I'll tell you what, man . . . you've shown the white feather, and you're in the hollow of my hand!"

"Watch me, then, open the fingers," Collier declared.

"I'm waiting, and watching," the sheriff said, setting his teeth and freshening his grip on the handle of the Colt.

"Your gun doesn't trouble me," said Collier. "If you were to shoot me, Sheriff, it would do you no good."

"No?"

"No, it would only hang you by the neck. There's no man in the world more safe than I am in your hands."

"Of course you're safe," the sheriff replied. "Safe for the jail, the jury, the judge, and the rope that'll hang you, Gadsden."

But plainly he was worried as he spoke. He had the hunted look of a fighter who seems to have the battle in his hands, and yet, dreading the cunning and the resource of his enemy, hesitates to step in and strike the finishing blow.

No wonder. If the prisoner had been Gadsden, how could Lassiter be sitting here, triumphant?

Hugh said calmly: "I'll tell you, Sheriff

40

Lassiter, the more famous you are, the faster with guns, the surer with weapons, the better I like it."

"Because of the glory you'll have in taking my scalp, Gadsden, is that it?"

"Because," Collier answered, "I'm simply safer in your hands."

Lassiter winced a little. "Go on," he said. "I'm waiting for the climax."

"It's as simple as the day. You must have guessed it yourself, man. I'm not Gadsden."

Lassiter started. The quickness of his intaken breath made him straighten in his chair.

"Oh," he said, "that's it, is it? You're not Gadsden?" He laughed a little, a brooding and fierce sound.

"Go on, Gadsden. Talk! Talk yourself out of my hands!"

"You've been close enough to see Gadsden's face," Collier insisted.

"Aye. Close enough to see his face, but never very clear. But, you dolt, don't you suppose the entire world knows the scar that runs down your face?"

"How was it made?" asked Collier

"The knife stroke the Mexican gave you, of course. That story's well enough known, also. You've been a perfect self-advertiser, Gadsden. What do you gain by it except cheap notoriety."

"A knife makes a steady cut," Collier said. "Lean a little closer and you'll see that the mark on my face is a dotted line. I got it from barbed wire. Lean closer and look straight at it, and then ask me if a knife ever could have made such a dotted line as that scar?"

V

The scar which appeared so plainly when Collier flushed was, under ordinary circumstances, by no means so clear, and the sheriff leaned close and closer still, studying the character of the white line that streaked down the face of the other.

And as he did so, a sudden thought leaped into the mind of Collier.

He could see that his previous conversation had unsteadied the mind of the sheriff. Simple truth, be it ever so much a matter of mere words, carries with it a stamp and brand of reality which fiction cannot match, and the shock of this quiet sincerity had made a definite impression upon Lassiter. His keen glance had quite failed to penetrate to any hidden mystery in the manner of Collier, for the very good reason that no mystery was there. And now, as he leaned forward to study the dim line of the scar, Collier could hardly fail to notice two things—a mental uncertainty revealed in the whole attitude of the other, and the significant fact that his right hand was loose—very loose—upon the Colt that he held. The gun itself had swerved a little to the side, so that it bore, Collier thought, outside the line of his body.

And as he perceived these things, temptation took him by the throat so violently that he choked, and his very body trembled with the force of it. Yonder stood his sullen friends, they who had peered at him with an excited and affectionate eagerness when they entered the dining room. Yonder stood Jack, the cook, at the kitchen door, pasty-faced and agape. There was pretty Molly, too, with her hands gripped hard as though she, at least, were contemplating an attack on the intruders. All these people had been to Collier as clansmen to their chief, but now they remained amazed and bewildered, for they had seen their hero sit quietly in place and allow himself to be covered and rendered helpless by a single warrior.

What would the real Gadsden, the great Gadsden, have done in such a case?

Certainly, he now would far rather die than allow his friends to look down upon him as a failure and a fraud. Another moment and the sham of the usurper would be exposed, they would scorn and laugh at this man they had been worshiping before. The sneer with which they had first looked upon Collier would return to their lips.

He knew it, and though a moment of reflection would have led him to see that what had leaped into his mind was entirely mad, yet he could not resist the temptation.

His left fist jumped to the chin of Lassiter, driving his head far back, and as the gun exploded in the sheriff's hand, Collier wrenched it from him.

An automatic fighting sense and ancient fighting skill still made Lassiter formidable. His left hand was flicking a heavy Colt into action when Collier smote again with the barrel of the gun he held straight into Lassiter's face, and the man of the law went down.

These actions had consumed, perhaps, the fifth part of a second, enough to make the posse men wheel about, and at the flash of their guns Collier knew that he was no better than a dead man if he remained there another moment. Foolish impulse had made him do a perfectly silly thing. Fear for his life made him move now.

The window was open beside him. Through it he bounded, with fear making his legs strong.

And something whiplashed through the hair of his head as he fell. A bullet, he knew.

He darted to the right around the corner of the building, thereby shutting himself off from the uproar of gunshots and furious voices, so that it sounded all at once dim and far away.

Dim and far away it was to Collier, also, for the instant he had leaped into the dying light of the outer day it seemed to him that within the dining room of the hotel had passed a brief and strange nightmare.

It was not he, Hugh Collier, who fled down the street for his life—he who never had broken even a whisper of the law before, except on that one unlucky occasion of the melon-stealing that had branded him for life. He felt a vast impulse to turn about and rush back into the place, holding his arms above his head to show that he had come in peace. He wanted to go back like that and yell to them that he had been mad. He had struck the man of the law. He would submit freely to whatever punishment must be inflicted, but under the heavy shadow of the law he must not rest.

Yet he dared not obey that sensible impulse. Would they not shoot him down, unquestioning, the instant they saw him coming? Dared he ever face the panther-like speed and the panther-like fury of the great Lassiter?

Even the real Gadsden might well have paused before doing such a thing, and when Collier contemplated it, he had an empty heart.

So he swerved around the corner of the building and came upon a group of horses standing with thrown reins—the horses of the posse, left here unguarded. Aye, placed straight in the path of Collier.

He did not have to choose among them, because the choice was thrust bodily upon him. A tall gray animal, with black stockings and black muzzle, looked the peer of all the rest. He flung himself awkwardly into the saddle, scooping up the reins, and the horse did the rest. It fled like a deer, straight across the road, plunging toward the trees beyond.

To the left lay the hotel, with armed men rushing out from it, one of them with a crimsoned face, who he took to be Lassiter certainly and no other. Their rifles went up. They yelled as they saw him darting off on the gray. Perhaps their rage unsettled their aim, for none of the singing wasps that filled the air stung Collier. Then the thick, safe shadow of the woods covered him.

Straight up the winding trail he flew until the gray faltered a little against the heaviness of the slope. Then Collier pulled him to the side among the trees and slid to the ground.

He hardly could have sat the saddle another minute. He was weak as water, trembling as air, so that he flung an arm over the pommel of the saddle, then leaned his weight against the good horse.

No man coming to himself with a memory of what he had done in a mad fit could have shuddered more than Collier did now. He felt his past life reeling back from behind him as trees and telegraph poles fly away past the windows of a speeding train. That safe little town of Stanton where he always had lived—where he always expected to live—now dissolved into a dim mist, rose like dust in the wind, disappeared.

All the faces of his friends flew past him like doves dropping down the wind. All the years of his life fled away and rattled as dead leaves in the air.

He would go back, he told himself. Even yet it was not too late. He would redeem and reclaim the old life, instead of allowing himself to be thrust out like this into the empty coldness of a new existence for which he was not prepared.

But here he heard the pounding of hoofs, the calling of men's voices.

One ringing note sounded above the rest, shrilling to his companions to spread out to the right, some to keep the trail, others to the left. Still yelling commands, the voice bore down upon Collier, who stood transfixed. He could no more have moved than a wooden image, or a snowman. But feeling that his fate was plunging upon him, he resigned himself.

Strange thoughts leaped through his mind at that instant. When they sent him to the prison it would be as a resister of arrest, as one who had made an assault upon a duly constituted officer of the law, beyond that, as a horse thief! The penalty for this was heavy. How many years? Five? Ten? Fifteen?

Yonder in the town of Stanton men and women would not greatly care, for in the placid, dream-like course of his life he had formed no vital friendships. His going would be neither a shadow nor a touch of sun for any human being. There was no father, no mother, no brother, no kin however distant to wail for him. The Stanton papers would duly note his downfall from among the ranks of the law-obeying, not because he was of the slightest importance, but because he had come from that small city. He saw the president of the bank, the acid mouth of the keeper of the boarding house, the good broad grin of the janitor, the bewildered, puckered face of old Miss Simmons, who had been his teacher in the fifth grade and still vaguely remembered him, vaguely smiled at him when she passed him on the street.

That was the last thought in the mind of poor Hugh Collier when the horseman leaped through the woods, and he saw it was Lassiter in person bearing down. He looked no longer small, but giant-large, with a poised revolver in his hand, and his red face contorted to an inhuman mask.

Collier did not prepare to die. He neither fled nor drew himself up, but he blinked like an owl and waited without a thought to be shot through the heart.

Instead, the wild rider rushed on past him, to be soaked up instantly among the shadowy trees!

Only then did Collier realize the dimness of the light, together with the importance of keeping perfectly still in the open if one wishes to remain unseen. But the terrible sheriff had gone rushing on up the mountainside, and again his voice sounded, pinched thin and high with his unflagging rage!

What that rage must be, Collier could well imagine. Such a thing was more incredible than any page of a story book—that the famous Lassiter had been struck down, his weapon taken from him, and the criminal had escaped after being closely covered by Lassiter's own gun!

It made poor Collier dizzy to think of it.

He was deeply grateful that he had been spared to live beyond the first fury of the sheriff. And he saw at once what he must do.

He would return through the dusk to the barn, slip in quietly, steal out the bay gelding to which he had a right, leave this stolen animal in its place, and instantly ride off down the mountain slope toward Stanton. Let blessings fall upon the moment that saw him safely within the familiar precincts of that place.

He started at once, and, riding the horse in a semicircle, he crossed the road well below the town, came up behind it, and easily got to the hotel stable through the copse at its rear. It was almost utter dark, now. He led the captured horse into the thick of the shadows inside the barn until his outstretched hand touched the hip of a horse whose hair was stiffened with the salt of dried sweat: That should be the gelding that fairly belonged to him.

He spoke to it softly, just as something was jammed against his back.

"Stand mighty still," said a voice at his ear, "or I'll pulverize your spine for ye!"

VI

As a half-stunning blow causes darts and sparkles of red to dance before the eyes, so that unexpected voice made gleams of light spring up across the mind of Collier, but his first thought was that he had been a fool, a gross fool, to return for the horse. He should have gone by foot straight down from the mountains toward that dull town of Stanton where, nevertheless, was doubly blessed peace.

"Yank up yer hands!" commanded the captor. "Here, Bud, show a light."

A lantern shutter clicked and a strong ray touched a big cobweb on the rafters overhead, then wavered down and steadied upon the face of Collier. An exclamation from two voices instantly followed.

"Gadsden!"

Then, as the lantern was fully exposed, he saw that the bearer of it was none other than the messenger who had brought him word of the coming of Lassiter—a year, it seemed, since that meager, quick-stepping fellow had come into the dining room.

"The chief!" the other said, and moving back with a start, he revealed himself to Collier as one of those who had trooped into the hotel to survey him with friendly admiration.

"Damned sorry," he said anxiously, throwing a sawed-off shotgun under his left arm. "Might of knowed that you'd come back, chief. Here, lemme put up the horse. Lassiter's horse! Bud, look here! It's Lassiter's gray!"

He burst into jubilant laughter, while Bud came up eagerly to stare at the animal.

"Lassiter'll go pretty nigh mad," said Bud. "Knocked down and made a fool of, and his horse took right under his eyes. He'll be frothin' at the mouth, I reckon!"

They led the gray into the adjoining stall and took the saddle from its back while Collier stood by, uncertain as to what he should do next. It was well enough to have been spared the charge in the big barrels of the shotgun, of course, but he wanted desperately to get away from these overly friendly ruffians. Among these men who called him "chief" there surely was one who knew the face of the real Gadsden.

The instant that fellow appeared, the sham would be exposed.

"Lassiter's done for," declared the man with

51

the shotgun. "He's been made a fool of with twenty gents lookin' on. Him that's been ragin' and rampagin' up and down the range. He's got his face marked for himself, too. I wondered why you didn't slam a bullet through his brains, chief," he said respectfully to Collier, "but I reckon I know why. Death'd be no punishment for him . . . what he's done. He's gotta live and see people grin when he goes by. That'll be poison for him, all right. His horse gone, too!"

He laughed through his teeth with excess of ferocious joy.

"I'm taking out the bay," Collier said in a matter-of-fact tone.

"You ain't gonna start out now," protested Bud.

"I've got to start now," declared Collier.

"Wait a minute! Not now! What'll the boys do if they miss you? They wanna see you bad. They got things to say to you . . . will you only come around for a minute, chief?"

Each of them possessed himself of one of Collier's arms, and he could not help being led from the barn and into the hotel dining room, where he found a swirling, confused crowd.

Out of that mob, at the sight of him, there went up a shout that half deafened him.

"Clean out everybody except them that belong!" thundered someone. "Pull the shutters close. He's come back. Hey! Gadsden's back with us!"

Some drove from the room the men and children who did not belong to the selected group. Others surrounded Collier in a joyous circle.

After that first explosion of joy, their voices were lowered. Still their wild, brown faces were alight. They smote one another on back and shoulder. They chuckled deep in their throats. They gazed on Collier with a consuming admiration that came from their very hearts, it was apparent.

It did not appear to be that the sheriff's discomfiture had pleased them so much as the manner of it. How Collier had remained quietly in his chair waiting for the man of the law to come, and how he had submitted to being under the drawn gun, and how he had sat coolly chatting with that formidable enemy, face to face. These things delighted them, and they talked of it in broken phrases, interrupted with huge, complicated curses. They were amazed that, when the fight came, their chief had not put a bullet through the head of the sheriff, but had preferred to let him live. It was a subtlety of torment, a peculiar insolence of power that pleased them to the very cockles of their beings.

It was a thought which would not have occurred to them, and for that very reason it pleased them the more!

From their talk he gathered other details of his

supposed character. And of the reason for the appearance of "Gadsden" here.

A former leader of these men—outlawed robbers it appeared that most of them were—had been captured by that same alert spirit of trouble, Lassiter. So an appeal had been sent out to the great Gadsden, and, behold, he had come a long distance to appear among them as their new chief. Gadsden with the scarred face—he was the man!

That made it simple why they had mistaken him, going by the sole mark of the scar. Gadsden, then, was the rider of the bay gelding. Gadsden was he who had made the change of mounts, and thereby shifted Lassiter's pursuit onto another trail. A cunning fellow, that Gadsden, a man as clever as he was strong and fierce. Presently he would return from the wilderness to thrust out the impostor who pretended to his place. Another forcible reason, if other reasons were needed, why Collier must fly from this unlucky spot at once.

Hugh still wondered a little how he could have been mistaken for one who in nearly every respect was clearly different from him. They were merely of a type, and somewhere near the same age. Otherwise no one could have confused them together.

It was only the scar that had singled him out, and the horse on which he had ridden into the town. Those slight chances doubtless had been foreseen by the true Gadsden, who now laughed securely somewhere in the background, preparing to come and take his own at leisure. Certainly, Collier had no mind to thwart him. His heart turned cold at the mere idea. And yet he was delighted with the adulation of this crowd of mountaineers as nothing in his life ever had delighted him before.

One step, now, and he would sever his connection with this tangled affair. It would lie behind him as an oasis of excitement in a dull life.

They were apologizing to him, now, because they had allowed him to be cornered and made helpless, to all appearances, by the sheriff. But if he had given one sign—one signal for which they had been waiting desperately—they would have swept the sheriff and his posse from the place, or died trying!

Now these voices sounded quietly and rapidly in the ear of Collier, and he knew that the speakers meant what they said. There was more sheer manhood gathered about him than he ever had seen before in all his life, and he could have laughed aloud when he thought that there was not a man in the number who could not strike harder, ride better, last longer, shoot straighter, run faster, jump farther than could he. And every one of them, now looking up to him as a peerless chief and leader, was infinitely superior to him in every one of the respects for which they held him in their admiration. Their brown faces, lean and hard with constant outdoor exposure, their wide, sinewy shoulders, their straight-looking eyes, filled him with both awe and admiration, but he could only accept their adulation without criticizing it. What if he told them that he was not the great Gadsden at all, but only a bungling bank clerk of no importance, out for a vacation? They would take it as a clumsy lie, for had they not seen him confound the great Lassiter himself?

That mad impulse, that single wild action, was enough to give this dream reality in the days to come if only he could escape now from the tangle in which he was caught.

Bud—that small man filled with fire as a sheath is filled with the sword blade—stood before him with a smile of admiration, almost of affection.

"Tell us why you done it, chief? Why didn't you plaster him with a Forty-Five-caliber slug?"

How could Collier confess that the blow had been struck in desperation, without forethought, merely with a desire to beat down this dangerous man?

He could only say: "Lassiter's a good fellow in his way. . . ."

"In the killing way!" exclaimed Bud. "That's the way that he's good!"

What reason should Collier give?

"What's the reason to be a cat if there isn't a dog to chase you?" he asked.

He was ashamed of such a silly reply, but the others did not seem to notice anything unusual in it except its insolent insouciance.

They dwelt upon his last words as they had dwelt upon his face, in wonder and delight.

"A few less dogs, chief, if you please," Bud said, laughing. "Or let 'em be dogs with fewer teeth than Lassiter. He's had us all runnin' up trees, now and then!"

The others agreed as well, but they agreed with laughter that trailed off to a sudden murmur. Word came in swiftly from the door.

"She's here!" someone said to Collier.

"Kate Memphis is here," said another.

"Who?" Collier repeated blankly.

"Jack Memphis's daughter," said Bud. "Her that he's made the fine lady out of. Here's Kate now!"

Other voices murmured other things, but Hugh Collier did not hear them clearly, only phrases and detached words.

"Harder than she looks."

"Oak with a velvet finish."

"Knows horses."

"The old man's kid!"

"Straight!"

He gathered such phrases, such words as these from the muttering around him, but all his senses were employed on his own behalf in watching her.

For she was a golden beauty, and as she stood in the doorway against the black of the night, she glowed to the eye of Collier like a pearl cupped in a dusky hand.

VII

He could not say that she was either tall or short, but her size was right for Collier. He could not say that her hair was auburn or gold, for the glow of it was what he watched. Her eyes might be gray or blue, but all that Collier sensed was the curiosity, the fear, and the hope in them as Bud, ever ready to do the right thing, brought her forward to him.

"Here he is, Kate. Here's Bill Gadsden come to fix everything up. Shake hands with the new chief."

She reached out her hand slowly, so busy was she in studying his face. It seemed to Collier that a shadow of doubt and suspicion came over her own for the moment as she looked at him.

"I heard you were here," she said. "I came to thank you for coming to help my father. I heard that you'd met Lassiter, too. And that you'd beaten him."

He watched her hand grip into a fist as she

said this. Up into Collier's throat came rushing the admission that he was not Gadsden but only a very confused and uncertain fellow, a tenderfoot of the tenderest variety. But the words died unspoken. He knew, as he looked down at her, that however he must work to serve her imprisoned father, whatever he must pretend, however great must be the sham, he would not leave his assumed self until he was forced to do so. From that instant he commenced to live the lie!

For the lie in itself was his hold upon her. It was what had brought her to him on this night, and what would unite them again in the future. No matter how precarious that connection might be, how likely to be destroyed in one touch by some clownish exhibition of his own incompetence, by the coming of the true Gadsden, by the warrior hand of Lassiter, or by the challenge of some far lesser man, still he knew that he could not give up this slim opportunity of appearing before her as a great man for a little while. Bitterly he admitted his weakness, but his heart leaped at the thought of the days that might come.

So her hand left his, and he was saying: "About Lassiter . . . the luck was with me. About your father . . . why, I'll do what I can . . . I and the rest of the boys."

"We'd better get out of here," Bud advised. "Lassiter and his gang may circle back here any time. I'm gonna take him up to my place tonight. Come over in the mornin', and we'll talk. Don't you worry, because he'll crack the jail like a soft-shelled almond. He can do it! He cracked Lassiter wide open, like you never seen a man handled."

"I wish I'd seen it," she said. "The scoundrel. Ah, the treacherous, bloodthirsty scoundrel!"

Bud jumped on a chair.

"Scatter and spread out, boys," he said. "There ain't any use of stayin' here except to draw trouble thicker'n flies. Scatter out, and I'll pass you the sign from the hill head above my shack when you're wanted. Get out! We gotta move! Hey, Lefty . . . you and Mart see Kate home, will you?"

There was instant action. The crowd dissolved. What Collier remembered was the smile of Kate Memphis as she watched him over her shoulder, departing. And he wanted to pursue her, but that he could not do without finding more to say, and no more words came, only a guilty joy at the sight and at the thought of her.

It was after this that he saw the plump face of Jack, the cook, with Molly grinning close by him.

"Great Scott!" exclaimed Collier. "I haven't paid for my dinner! What's the bill, Molly?"

"It blew out the window," she answered. "The Lassiter gang's bullets carried it away with them, and I can't write another."

"You can't pay in this here house," Jack said

gravely. "What kind of folks you think we are, anyway?"

"Come on," agreed Bud. "We better slide out. They'll get their share out of us, before the finish."

He led the way out to the horses. Both the bay that the real Gadsden had traded to Collier, and the taller gray horse that he had taken from the posse's line, were in place before the hotel, someone having attended to their saddling at the direction of Bud, it appeared.

Then in another moment Collier was on the back of Lassiter's own horse, heading up the road with his companion, the tired bay gelding on a lead rope behind the latter's mustang.

It was like saying a farewell at a dock, a stepping up the gangplank, a casting off of mooring cables, the tooting of raucous horns, but now at last the departure had been taken, and Collier was committed to a wide and strange sea of danger, where many reefs, he knew, lay in his path, though they were uncharted.

Yet he was not so downhearted as he had expected to be. Out of the evergreens came a wind of wonderful sweetness, and the great mountain stars shone bright and close above the summits. If it had been even a dull scene, the cheerful voice of his companion would have been enough to raise the spirits of Collier. For to Bud it seemed that the fight already was ended.

"There's Lassiter slapped in the face, beat and done . . . what a slick short left you hung on his chin, old-timer! That'll buck up the boys a pile. There's no better way of showin' that a horse can be rode than by stickin' in the saddle on him. They ain't a thing in the world that'll draw the lads together so much as the knowin' that you've handled that Lassiter. They been pretty bad staggered. They've fell off a lot since Memphis went down."

"How did it happen?" asked Collier.

"Lassiter! That's the what and how. He's enough to happen to pretty nigh anybody, except a Gadsden. A gent that's beat and down, he don't look so hard to the one that dropped him, but he might clean up the rest of the world. Only the champion can beat the best contender. Don't make no mistake about Lassiter. He's hard. He's sharp as a needle and he never gets dull. Even if he failed to get under your skin. I tell you how big he is when I tell you about Memphis. You know about Memphis?"

"I've heard of him, of course."

That was true enough. But Hugh had thought that Jack Memphis was rather a legend than a fact—one of those figures dimly nestled away in the arms of tradition, without any true reality emerging. Jack Memphis, like a Norse god, was wrapped in mists of narrated fancies from which only now and again the shining truth emerged.

Bandit with a sense of humor, robber with good grace, land pirate with a heart of mercy, leader of far worse men than himself, he had impressed young minds and old as a sort of Robin Hood of the mountains. In that role, Collier had heard of him from his boyhood.

"You've heard a lot about him," Bud explained, "but nothin' likely that matches up with the truth. But I've seen him when he was young and prime. I've seen him lift a thousand pound of cast-iron junk and put it on the weighin' scales in a sack. There ain't any joke about that, mind you. I've seen him when he was quicker than a wildcat . . . quick as you, Gadsden, pretty nigh, even though I seen you make your two-handed play for Lassiter's gun and jaw at the same time! That was pretty hard to beat, but old Memphis was in your class. Maybe the years have slowed him up a mite. It takes a stake horse to give away pounds, and a great man to give away too many years. But the boys and me, we used to watch him and it didn't seem to us that he'd turned brittle any, in spite of the gray on the sides of his head."

"How old is he?"

"Forty-five, maybe. But now along comes Lassiter. He tries three or four times to get at Jack Memphis, and he misses every time, and finally he snags Mike Oliver. Gets him in a fair stand-up fight, and shoots Mike down with a slug through the leg. Takes him up, gets him healed, sends him right on into the mountains, clean free . . . and Mike with a killin' on his hands, to say nothin' of a couple of safe-crackin's and such."

"How could a sheriff turn loose such a man, Bud?"

"You might ask, old-timer. So did the rest of us, but Lassiter ain't the kind that angles for the little fish. He wants the game more than he wants the dead ones. So he sends Mike loose and free when he's well enough to ride, and all for the sake of makin' Mike his messenger. Mike comes into camp one evenin' . . . mighty well I remember it . . . and he sets down and lets us gape at him like fish out of water. I was sure surprised. I reckoned that they'd of had a rope fitted to the size of Mike's collar, by that time! Then Mike up and tells us the story . . . how Lassiter had taken care of him, and how he was turned loose, and all that he had to do was to come up to the camp and tell the chief that on the Kirby trail a week from that day Lassiter would be waiting for him, to give him a fair break and a fair chance at guns. Otherwise, if Memphis didn't want to take that chance, he ought to send back Mike to him.

"Which we all listened to this and figured that it was fair and square. Mike, especially, he seemed to think it was all right, because none of us dreamed that even Lassiter would have a stand-up chance ag'in' Jack Memphis.

"We was wrong!"

"It was a fair fight?" Collier asked, knowing the answer to the question even as he asked it.

"As fair as you ever seen! I was a quarter of a mile off, on the edge of the woods, with a strong pair of glasses turned bang on Jack Memphis, when I seen Lassiter ride out of a tuft of poplars beside of a creek.

"They talked for a minute, what nobody could hear, and then they went for their guns with one whack of their hands. Both them guns spoke, but Lassiter had the first bullet in. Why, he must of beat Jack on the draw by as much as a tenth part of a second, which is a terrible long ways, when it comes to figuring up.

"Down went Jack Memphis tumblin' out of the saddle and layin' limp and loose in the dust of the road. It made me pretty sick to see that. He was drilled clean through the body, and he's been sick these here weeks, till he was strong enough to get to his trial. But it wasn't the idea of him bein' wounded or dead that hurt us all so bad. It was seein' that a great man like Jack Memphis could come to his finish at last and meet a better man than himself."

He threw up his hands as he spoke.

"We've had the starch took out of us, since then. Some of the boys have faded away. Loomis, he went to Canada. Craig started for the Río. Ham Butterworth got into cow-punchin' ag'in. And the rest of us ain't had no heart, till we thought of sendin' for you and askin' you to come down and head the old crew."

Collier hardly heard the last words. He was thinking too busily of that picture of the deadly Lassiter waiting in the road, and he himself riding down to meet his certain fate.

VIII

The moon came up while they still were on the road. It made the mountains more wildly remote and huge. It painted them in black, deep as soot, but struck them here and there with relieving lines, like dull silver gilt. Those were the cliffs of massive and polished rock, and high above, glimmering in the ghostly light, they could see the regions of the snow, sometimes looking like clouds in the sky. But the mountains became more gloomily romantic under the moon.

It was not the first time that Collier had seen it rise through the eastern trees, like a body of pale flame that, at length, detached itself from the tops of the pines and then floated away into the deep dark of the sky, instantly becoming as remote as the stars themselves. But, on the other nights, he had seen this from the secure warmth of his blankets, and had been quietly grateful that he could lie in comfort while the beasts of prey slipped abroad from shadow to shadow, and while the men of prey also rode forth from their fastnesses to evil deeds. But he, together with all honest and timorous souls, remained in the shelter of his blankets and could faintly smile at the other dangers.

He could smile no longer, for he was himself drawn out into the very world that he had wondered and shuddered at. Out of ourselves we paint all things that are around us. To the happy man they are bright, and to the sad man they are dark. Certainly on this evening it appeared to Collier that the pines on either side of the trail were black giants with arms raised to forbid his passing. And sometimes they rode through a double row so solidly set that the moon could not send its light through the interstices between the trees, and all was solid darkness about them, with the treetops fencing through the sky a ragged road. Or, again, where the growth was more open, they had glimpses of dim glades, and they heard the light voices of the water bubbling and singing, while it flashed and leaped beneath the moon. All the world was turned into an unearthly realm, for Collier, and he wondered at it with a chilly spirit. There was beauty here, but there was terror also, poisoning the loveliness. It needed some rougher spirit, some Gadsden, some Lassiter, some Jack Memphis to ride through scenes like these and enjoy them with an unperturbed spirit, but as for lesser souls like his own, they could not help but quail.

He observed after a time that his companion had grown silent and continually stole puzzled glances at him. At last, as they trotted down a slope, the curiosity of Bud could be contained no longer, and he broke out.

"Since you was laid up, chief, I reckon it's spoiled the pleasure of ridin' for you a pile."

At this reference to his horsemanship, Collier was glad of the dim light to cover his blush. He had almost forgotten that his greenness was bound to be observed almost instantly in the saddle. At the same time, there appeared a loophole of escape. He had been ill, it appeared, for he surmised that from the "laid up" comment of his companion.

And he said: "I'll tell you how it is, Bud. Since I was laid up a while, I've never felt at home in the saddle."

"No?" Bud said sympathetically.

They had entered one of the dark passages, and Collier, remembering the centaur-like figure which Gadsden had presented when in the saddle, could afford to smile without secrecy.

"In fact," he continued, "I've been feeling quite out of place on the back of a horse."

The pause of Bud plainly indicated that he was fighting against surprise and disappointment, but he almost immediately covered this pause by saying, with hasty loyalty: "Well, you've had yours, old son! Anybody that gets it through the middle of his dinner has gotta feel changed in his inside and in his head, for a while."

It appeared, from this, that the redoubtable Gadsden actually had recovered after being shot through the stomach, or at least, in the vicinity of it. But Bud was not content with this remark. He continued, in order to make his new friend and leader feel more at ease.

"There was Hal Storey. I knew Hal when he wouldn't look at a horse that didn't have kinks in it big enough to break a leg over. If you seen a fine, upstandin' horse that knew good manners and was dog-goned proud of what he knowed, a horse that could run a mile in nothin' flat, maybe, and do it without spilling water out of a glass balanced on the pommel . . . if you know what I mean. . . ." He paused for breath.

"Yes?" Collier said politely.

"Why, this here Storey, I'm telling you about, he went to sleep when he seen a fine horse like that. And when he packed his rope out to the corral to rope out a string for himself, if he seen a Roman-nosed fool tryin' to stand on his head or kick down the side of the barn, he was plumb tickled and dropped his noose on that cayuse, and called it his own. If he couldn't begin a day with ten minutes of danger to warm him up, he didn't feel real good, and run down on his appetite. Of course, he got throwed, and had his legs busted half a dozen times, so's when he walked, it was hard to tell whether he minded to go straight ahead or go wobblin' sideways, like a crab. He was raked off on fences, and bumped off on trees, and pitched on his head, and slammed on his back, and sat hard on his rear end. He was doubled up, and he was flattened out. He had a horse dance on him after he was down, and he'd been chewed a coupla times, too, till the horse found it didn't like the taste of that kind of meat, and spat him out, as you might say. But finally along comes a day when this here Storey was draped over a barbed-wire fence, and he come to kickin' himself in the nose with his own boots. You see, the wire, it had sawed through his coat and shirt and was workin' gradually into his insides.

"So Storey, he dragged himself off of that wire just before it finished partin' him in two halves, and right from that day to this, he ain't had a hankerin' for a buckin' horse, or a pitchin' cayuse, or anything of that kind, as you might say. But you give him a dog-goned old sleeper with no more than one eye open at a time, and he picks out that bronc and goes out to work raisin' the dust at every step. Storey has come down in the world, and he don't get close enough to a cow to daub on his rope more than a coupla times a season. Not meanin'," added Bud with fervent haste, "that you've come down in the world, because with my own eyes I see you whang Lassiter on the chin, and take his gun away from him like it was bad medicine for a boy of his age. I was only aimin' to tell you how it happens with gents that I've knowed, now and then. But you'll come back, chief, and one of these here days, you'll ride the way you done that day when you went clean from Helena to Butte with two cracked ribs and a broke collar bone! Speakin' personal, if I'd had the designin' of a man, I'd of give him a collar bone ten times the size of what he's fixed up with."

"Helena to Butte," Collier murmured, more and more appalled by the famous things which Gadsden had accomplished in his life. "Ah, yes!"

"Sure, that was a ride!"

"You've heard about it down here?"

"Why, folks talked about it for years. They talked about nothin' you did, more than that, except that maybe it was the time that you met up with the four Canucks that figured on takin' the right of way!"

Here Collier's companion broke into a gale of hearty laughter.

"But while you was finishin' them off," Bud said, "I never got the straight of it. Did you brain that last gent with his own gunstock, or did you shoot him?"

"Why, it's a long time ago," Collier said stiffly.

"Not meanin' any offense," declared Bud. "Except that some day when you're feelin' talky, I'd like to learn how you come out with them two Mexicans that time when you got your face slashed."

Four Canucks—two Mexicans—what a terror of a man this Gadsden appeared to be, for sure! But there was nothing that Collier could say in answer, except to mutter that things that were done were finished.

"It's all right," Bud said. "They's some talk about everything they've done, free and liberal. It makes 'em feel good. And they's some that only talk to old friends, and they's some that don't waste words on nothin' and nobody at all. We better head off right here."

He led the way on his little mustang through the woods, until the trees grew less thickly placed, and finally thinned out to a natural clearing, in the midst of which stood a small cabin. In the lean-to behind this they quartered their horses, and Bud brought out a supply of crushed barley that the animals were fed. The men stood by for a moment to watch them eat.

"Which would beat?" murmured Bud at length. "Lassiter's gray or your bay, chief? But that ain't never gonna be decided no more, because they both belong to you. If he ain't bawlin' after that horse tonight like a cow after its calf, I'm an Apache and never been called Bud."

They went into the house where Bud hospitably offered a drink of moonshine. "Sure good and mellow, partner, because it's been aged three whole months in the wood. Look how yellow it is from the charcoal!" But even this extremely matured liquor was refused by Collier.

For he was desperately weary from the physical labor and the mental strain of this long day. He was brought, accordingly, into one of the two small rooms of which the shack was composed, and an Indian willow bed was rolled down there for his comfort, with a straw mattress and comfortable blankets to be spread down on it.

"If you got any sleep in you, it'll sure come out when you lay down on that," said Bud. "They can have their springs and down and feathers and all that, but gimme a willow bed and half a chance is all that I say. Then I'll sleep! I'm bunkin' down in the next room. Make yourself plumb comfortable, and if they's anything that you lack, lemme know. I'll fetch it for you if I got it. We're gonna have the whole crew over here in the mornin' to talk over the job of gettin' Memphis out of the can. Not that it's possible. We all know that it ain't. A jail is one thing, but a state's prison is a long shot away from it!"

He went off to his own bed, and by the time that Collier had turned in, he could hear the steady snoring of his new friend.

Or dared he call any of these people his friends,

since all their loyalty was falsely held by him and really belonged to another man?

On this thought he fell asleep, and wakened, he knew not how much later, with a hand upon his shoulder.

IX

It was not Bud. In the first place, Collier still heard the snoring from the adjoining room.

In the second place, it was another presence, as he could guess with a strange prescience. Something far more formidable than Bud leaned above him. Lassiter? Lassiter, who might have followed him like a panther, and now like a panther come in the middle of the night?

Collier lay perfectly still, incapable, in fact, of movement.

"Are you awake, now?" asked a voice.

"Y-Yes," stammered Collier.

"Sit up, then. I'll give you a light to see by."

A match was struck on trousers, making the sound of the scratching a mere hiss, then the lantern on the wall was lighted, the chimney being worked up and down without noise. The flame then settled, extremely low, so that it was a mere blur against the form of the stranger, yet it revealed enough of his face, as Collier sat up, to show him that it was Gadsden himself.

Gadsden!

There was no weapon near to Collier. He would not have dared to touch one had it been near. In fact, there was no reason why he should fear this man, and yet he knew that the coming of the light had not diminished but increased the terror he had felt in the dark of the cabin.

The gunman, standing by the lantern with arms akimbo, was silent and motionless, for a time. Then he came toward the bed and sat down on his heels, his elbows across his knees, his hands clasped. A faint smile was on his lips as he watched the startled face of Collier.

"Well," he said, "you see where you are, stranger?"

"In Bud's house," assented Collier faintly.

"That ain't all. You need more light than you got here, I guess," went on the other. "But suppose that turning up the wick won't give you all the light that you need."

He remained for a time without speaking. They watched one another, Collier still frightened, to be sure, but feeling that his heart gradually decreased in the speed and the violence of its beating.

"In Bud's house, but whose boots are you in?"

"In your boots, Gadsden, eh?"

"You've found out my name pretty *pronto*. Suppose you tell me yours?"

"Collier. Hugh Collier."

"Collier, I'm mighty glad to know you."

He held out a lean, brown hand. And, when Collier accepted the grasp, he again was conscious of a power far in excess of his own.

"I'm glad to know you," Collier repeated, the formula coming slowly over his stiff lips.

"Well, you don't know me," Gadsden replied unexpectedly. "There are a few around here who could come to know me. But you're not one of them, Collier."

He ceased speaking, and still Collier was aware of the quiet, amused smile upon the lips of the stranger. It was as though he were a child, and the other a teacher mildly pleased by a youngster's ignorance.

What foolish answers might be extracted from him now?

"Who are you, Collier?"

"I? Well, I'm just Hugh Collier."

"You've told me that. And John Smith is John Smith, and Bill Jones is Bill Jones, but that doesn't tell me anything more about them. What part of the mountains were you raised in?"

"I wasn't raised in them."

"You don't say."

The smile was more obvious, now.

"I came from Stanton."

"What do you do there?"

"I work in a bank."

"President, eh?"

"No, I'm just a clerk."

"Well, well," replied the other, in mock surprise once more. "Just a clerk. And here you are in the mountains . . . do you know what you're doing?"

"Filling Gadsden's boots . . . if that's what you want me to say."

"I don't want you to say anything. I wouldn't force you a bit, Hugh, old fellow. But I'd like to ask a few more questions and have you answer them just as you see fit."

"All right," Collier said faintly. He was beginning to pant.

"I don't mean any harm to you . . . I think," Gadsden said thoughtfully.

"Thanks," breathed Collier.

"But after you found out who they took you to be, why didn't you run for it?"

"I did."

"As far as the barn?"

"Yes."

"I know about that. Then when they got you back into the house, why didn't you make a clean breast of things?"

"I don't know. I wanted to," Collier said slowly.

"Of course you wanted to. You're no wild desperado, Collier, I take it."

"Not a bit. I'm a peace-loving man."

"Softer, softer. We don't want to wake up our good friend Bud in the next room. But he's a grand sleeper, at that. Listen to him."

The snoring of Bud echoed and rumbled through the place. Sometimes it shrilled high in the air, and sometimes it seemed to roll up out of the ground.

And then Collier began to wonder at the ease with which Gadsden maintained his cramping position. The man's muscles must be made of iron.

"I couldn't sleep like that," said Gadsden, "if I knew that a lean and hungry fellow like Lassiter was on my trail, and now with a battered nose . . . which you gave him, Hugh!"

He tilted back his head and laughed without losing his balance. The man seemed to have the grace, the poise, the lithe strength of a great cat.

"A very startling thing, that," Gadsden said. "But one has heard of the cornered rat!"

He had seen through the desperation of Collier. The latter shrank, and felt his very soul growing smaller. This was no common gunfighter who crouched here, toying with him and the affairs of his poor soul.

"But even after that, you decided to run for it. And run you did . . . were caught in the barn . . . brought into the hotel to triumph, and there, at least, when you were finally about to make a break away or a confession . . . then what happened, Hugh?"

Collier shrugged and frowned down to the floor. Fear, for the first time, left his heart a little free, and was somewhat replaced by the warmth of anger. For he thought of the girl, and then he was struck with amazement when the uncanny Gadsden continued.

"Then she came in through the door, and Hugh Collier being young . . . and Hugh Collier being a man . . ." He paused, with his smile inviting Collier to finish the sentence, but though the latter was sufficiently amazed, still he did not respond at once.

Gadsden stood up.

"It's nothing to be ashamed of," he said. "It's the same cause that brought me down here. Not even from the sight of her, Hugh. Only a glance at a snapshot of her. And after that, when they sent for me, I could no more refuse to go to her than a duck can keep from going to the water."

He laughed again, silently, an art over which he appeared to have a perfect command.

"What will it be, old fellow?" he said then. "I'm under an obligation to you. I'll do what you say. You can slip away, now, to the horse shed, and take the bay horse with you back to Stanton. I wouldn't advise it, though. Your own horse is in front of the cabin, and you'd better take that one, because Lassiter is apt to be interested in anyone riding that same bay horse. And Lassiter, as you may partly have guessed before, is a fire-breathing fellow, if ever there was one. So if I were you, I'd go take that horse of yours and ride away and let Bud find me sleeping in this bed when he comes in, in the morning. Matters could soon be explained, I'm sure."

Still Collier was silent. There was nothing to do but to take the advice of Gadsden, yet he could not willingly say yes. He was tongue-tied.

"In that case," Gadsden said as gently as before, "you'd have to stay on here and do the work which I came to do, that is . . . run this crew of wild men who used to call Memphis their boss, keep Lassiter at arm's length, and finally win pretty Kate Memphis, if you can, by getting her father out of prison."

He ended his list without comment. No comment was needed, as Collier contemplated the ideas one by one. Lassiter—the prison—the wild men of Jack Memphis—not the least of these things could he manage.

Then he heard Gadsden continue in the same good-natured, argumentative tone: "You come from Stanton. I know that town. A fine, quiet place. A good place for fine, quiet young men like you, partner. Go back to Stanton. She's filling your eyes, now . . . Kate Memphis. Makes your heart ache a little. Makes you homesick to think about her. But she's bait in a trap that's all set, Hugh, and that's pretty sure to break your back."

He paused for an answer from Collier, but still no answer came, as that unlucky youth looked with blank eyes into the future.

Then Gadsden went on: "I'm mighty sorry that I tangled you up in this affair. But I was scratching for my life, when I ran into you. Another thing . . . it's easy for a girl to do the smiling and hard for a man to do the forgetting. But you'll forget, Collier. Pull yourself together. Your horse is outside the house. It'll take you back to safety. It'll take you away from these mountains and the mountain men, their guns, and all that."

He presented the other side of the picture suddenly.

"Or else get ready to ride down to the prison and take Jack Memphis out of it. I'll show you the way to do it, if you wish."

Collier took a deep breath and closed his eyes.

"Tell me!" he said.

X

Still Gadsden crouched on his heels, unwearied, uncramped by that stilted position, and he said: "You know how the prison lies?"

"No. I never saw it."

"It's built into the lake at the end of a narrow peninsula. On the high land at the shoulder of the spit are the machine guns. Three little houses that look like fools' caps on the three hills. A double searchlight is on top of each one . . . revolving lights to sweep every hollow of the land. And everything's naked . . . no trees, no brush for shelter. The machine-gunners have their practice hour every morning. They get the ranges of the landmarks, so that in case of need they can blow every living thing off the face of the ground. But once past the machine guns, you come to the outer walls, on Thursday night."

Collier opened his eyes suddenly.

"That's tomorrow!"

"Of course. Now, then, when you come to the outer wall you are carrying with you a light silk ladder, such as I've got with me now. Extremely light, but wonderfully strong. Fitted with grappling irons at one end. The lower portion of the walls is made of rough masonry. There you crouch until the appointed time, making sure that you flatten yourself against the ground so that when the searchlights sweep the wall from time to time you won't be seen. You wait there till one o'clock sharp. At that exact time a guard with whom I've had conversation unlocks the door of the Memphis cell and allows Memphis to tie him hand and foot.

"Then Jack Memphis takes the keys and goes out from the cell corridor into the inner ward. He has the key for that gate. He unlocks it and enters the outer ward. But he cannot go to the gate through the outer wall, because that gate is lighted and guarded all night. He crouches there and watches the sentinels who are walking up and down that outer wall. The moon is clear at that time, so that he can see them quite well. He waits for the moment when their backs are turned to him.

"You, in the meantime, have climbed up the lower slope of the outer wall, quickly but carefully, because although the stones are roughly set, they give you only a bare toe and finger hold. And if you fall, you have a broken head. However, you climb until you come to the surface of the polished wall. No finger or toe holds here, old fellow. You hang on as well as you can with one hand. With the other you throw up the grappling iron thirty feet to the top of the wall. Probably you fail five or six times. But when the irons fall back, be sure that they don't tap you on the head and knock you silly. Also be sure that they don't drop with a clang on the wall, because the sentinels on top are fellows with sharp ears . . . and there was a jail break only three months ago at that same place.

"Now, then, after several casts we'll hope that the grapples hold, and you climb up the ladder to the top of the wall. Watching your time, of course, because of those same sentinels. When that's accomplished, you lie flat on the top, so as to keep yourself as well concealed as possible. You throw down the end of the ladder, and Jack Memphis catches it and starts climbing up. If at this time the guards see you, you shoot them down, and with Memphis on the top of the wall, you both climb down as fast as you can to the outer side. If the alarm has been given, you still have one chance in a thousand to get through the machine-gun fire. If the alarm has not been given, you slip along and have one chance in ten of avoiding the searchlights and breaking through. . . ."

"But why not the water?" Collier gasped, his hair on end at this long recital of perils to be overcome.

"Because on the water," said the other, "guard boats are cruising about all night long, and their own searchlights are constantly sweeping the surface, beginning a little after dark."

Collier, opening his agonized eyes again, searched desperately the face of his companion, but found there only the small, cold smile of irony.

"And when you've come through with him," said Gadsden, "certainly you'll have a clear way to the girl. You'll have a perfect alibi, also, for everyone in the know will be ready to swear that Gadsden did the trick, and not Hugh Collier. The law won't be able to touch you. Lassiter won't be able to touch you, either. There'll only be one future danger."

"And that?"

"Gadsden himself. Mind you, the picture was enough, but since then I've seen the girl herself, and the picture didn't do her justice. There'll

84

still be the real Gadsden between you and a happy home, Collier. So that's the story brought down to an end. You may wonder why I offer to let you take my place and do the work that I'd outlined for myself. But it's because I feel that I owe you something. You've filled my shoes so well up to this time, that I can't help feeling that you deserve a chance to fill them for a while longer."

He had ended, and now he stood erect.

He did not need to help himself up with his hands, even after crouching all this time, but he rose lightly as if helped up by a strong grip. Such a man as this, no doubt, would have better than one chance in ten, daring the dangers of the program that had just been outlined. But as for his clumsy self?

"I'm not wanting to hurry you," Gadsden said, "but I might point out that Bud has stopped snoring."

Poor Hugh Collier, glaring at the wall, saw all that had been described to him in prospect as clearly as though he were at that moment clinging to the wall of the prison, with the grapples flung up high above his head.

He parted his lips to say no, but the voice would not come. At least, he could shake his head.

"Meaning that you don't want to go on this party, Collier?" asked Gadsden.

Collier suddenly stared straight at the speaker.

He saw once more that faint, sneering smile, and the blood rushed into his brain, and his eyes were obscured.

"No!" he gasped. "I'll take the long chance . . . and damn you, Gadsden!"

"Here," said the quiet voice of Gadsden, "is the ladder. And good luck to you, old son."

It dropped on the floor, white, soft, wonderfully slender, so that all its length made only a small armful.

Collier reached out to touch it. The instant that its soft strands were under his fingers, the instant that he saw the hooked talons of the grappling irons, he knew that he could never push the attempt to a conclusion. He knew, and wakened as if from a deep sleep.

"I was a fool, Gadsden," he said. "I can't do it. I haven't the courage, and I haven't the skill to do such a thing. I'd botch it like a coward right in the middle and spoil everything. Besides, it's not really a plan. It's a crazy idea. I don't think that even you could do it!"

He looked up from the silken ladder.

But Gadsden no longer was there. Only the pale, silent moonlight was sliding through the window by which, doubtless, Gadsden had made his escape. In the patch of light, Collier saw a broken willow broom lying on the floor, and a rag of sacking. And suddenly he felt that he was like those tawdry, ruined things. A useless man in the true world of men, such as existed here on the frontier of life.

He sprang up and hurried to the window, but when he leaned out from it, he saw nothing, he heard nothing. If the horse had previously been left near at hand, it had been removed, now. Yes, far away he thought that he heard a covert, stealthy sound of crackling twigs.

His lips parted instinctively to shout after Gadsden and bring him back.

But, at that moment, he heard a deep, sonorous, vibrant sound begin in the next room. Bud was snoring again, peacefully, dreaming nothing of what had happened here, and the fire through which the soul of Collier had been passed.

The latter drew back from the window with his call unsounded. Then he returned to the bed, where he lay alternately burned with a fever of shame, and then chilled with the cold of bitter fear.

The night went on slowly. And after a time, sleep came almost in spite of himself.

It was a night of fierce dreams in which he was climbing up inaccessible heights, slipping when in grasp of the top, and hurtling down through uncalculated spaces until the rocks crunched his frail body at the end of the fall. One blinding instant of pain—then, half roused from slumber, he would begin the ghastly dream again. Voices, finally, came softly into his consciousness, blurred and indefinite, but finally dissolving into words.

"Sure layin' late."

"Hear him groan!"

"Aye, and he's had things to make him dream bad."

"Wake him up?"

"Naw, let him sleep. He'll have trouble enough when he opens his eyes."

Collier opened his eyes with a sigh, and before him he saw Bud, together with a tall man, whose face was covered with two inches of rough, uncombed beard. It gave him the appearance of an owl with small eyes, a wise, cruel owl, now hungry for prey.

"Hello, chief," Bud said. "Here's Steve Marvin just come in. He's been hankerin' to meet you. This is Gadsden, Steve."

Heaving himself up on one elbow, Collier took the proffered hand, and saw the naked skin around the eyes of Marvin flush a deep red, so moved was he to meet the great man of the mountains.

He could not even speak, in answer to Collier's words, and Bud, with a laugh of understanding, pushed his companion toward the door.

"Steve is better with a Winchester than with words," he said. "You can bet on Steve in the pinches."

Then, as Marvin disappeared, he leaned closer

to add: "Been wantin' Steve with us for years, but he wouldn't come in till he heard that the real Gadsden was with us. Hurry up, chief, the gang is comin' in. Hurry along, and I'll have a bang-up breakfast ready for you. We're gonna eat before we talk."

Collier, as the other left, rose slowly from the bed. He knew what his talk would consist in—a simple and shameful confession of the sham part that he had been playing. Perhaps it was not too late to get the true Gadsden back for that night's work.

XI

He came out into the flush of the morning grim with his resolve, and found himself instantly standing straighter and breathing more deeply, for the pure air forced his shoulders back, and if anything could have raised his spirits, it would have been the thrill of bird song that lifted from the trees around the clearing. Through a rift he saw the ranges walk away from brown to blue, and far off, above them, a white giant barely visible through the morning mist.

As those mountains lifted above the plain, so these chosen spirits rose above common men, and as the great peaks ruled serene above the ranges, so were such warriors as Gadsden and Lassiter.

But he, Collier, who should be sheltered in some low valley—here he was placed on an eminence, with all the others looking up to him.

The men stood up from around the fire in the center of the clearing, over which a pair of pot-hangers arose. They stood up and turned toward him with a murmur of pleasure at his coming that was more from the heart than any cheer.

He advanced toward them with his resolve hardening upon him. He would tell them quickly, simply—ask them to forgive him—point out how he had been led forward from step to step by circumstance. As he came closer, his resolution was still firmer, for he could measure their manhood better when they were nearer by. Big men, almost every one, strong-boned, strong-muscled, but stripped clean of all fat by their vigorous lives, they were obviously each one chosen above a thousand. They waved their hands to him as he came up, and Bud was beginning the round of introductions. Diffidently they took his hand. They were like children, avoiding his eye a little, but eventually flashing up at him a keen, steady glance under which he could not help wincing. He had met the last of them, when a horse snorted in the woods and into the open pranced a high-headed mustang, slenderly beautiful as any deer, its crimson nostrils flaring, its eyes stained red with fiercely high spirits. There was no man on the back of this little tiger among horses, but Kate Memphis rode the mare with an easy, confident hand.

She swung down and threw the reins, coming straight forward to Collier.

Well, let her hear his renunciation of his false name, and his reassumption of his true one. After all, though it was bitter, Gadsden had been right. It was easy for a woman to smile and perhaps hard for a man to forget. But forget he could because forget he must.

He was glad that she was not brightly dressed to set her beauty off. But instead, she wore battered khaki—a divided skirt ripped by thorns and whipped by sharp-ended twigs, a shirt of the same material, a short coat unbuttoned, a big-brimmed hat that made her look smaller than ever. At a little distance she looked no more than a child. Only when she came closer he saw the details. There was a single touch of decoration. Her shirt was open at the throat, and where it divided she had pinned a spray of wild roses—something that she had broken off carelessly because it sprang up on the trail that she happened to follow that morning.

But Collier would have been glad if she had been adorned totally. The nightingale is a plain brown bird; it has only the gift of song. And the rose at her breast was in her cheeks, as well, and in the sky above them. She was like the morning itself as she smiled at poor Collier. Her hand clung to his hand for an instant, her eyes clung to his eyes.

All his resolution departed!

They breakfasted around the fire, she and Collier side by side, and the others keeping at a little distance, and maintaining a steady talk of their own, sufficiently boisterous and noisy to give privacy to his talk with Kate Memphis. He talked bluntly, because she seemed to stop up his avenues of thought and speech. What had she known of her father?

That he was a persecuted man.

"Persecuted?" echoed Collier.

"That's what my mother and I thought. He was, too, in the beginning. They accused him of cheating the bank where he worked. And he slipped into the mountains instead of standing trial. Afterward, it was made clear that he was perfectly innocent. By that time, there were other crimes lodged against him . . . robberies of a good many kinds. The president of the bank where he used to work managed to see him and told Father that all the other charges could be quashed, and invited him to come back to work for him. Not that he wanted him a great deal, I suppose, but because he was a just man."

"But your father didn't go?"

"No. I've heard the story a good many times, since then. While the banker was talking, one of the men came in with a deer behind his saddle, and another walked up with a long string of trout. 'You can't get these in a bank,' my father said. 'You only get the sight of short-horned loans and long-horned mortgages. You bag a few widows and a good many children in the course of your season. You're always open, and it's hard on the small game. I'm not going back. I'd rather take my chances with men, where they grow man-sized!' "

"That sounds well," Collier said, a little puzzled, nevertheless.

She balanced on her knees the big, clean chip of wood that served her as a plate and skillfully dissected a trout that had been laid hissing hot upon it.

"It's chiefly sound, more than fact," she admitted. "I don't want you to think that I've been hoping you'd help Father because he's been a good man. I know that he's lived by the hardness of his fist and the straightness of his shooting for a long time. I've had my eyes opened a good deal since I came here from school. Of course, the reason he did not want to go back to work was simply because that would have been drudgery. But I'd made him promise to give up this life, just before the end. Just before Lassiter . . ."

She stopped, and, raising her head a trifle, she looked full into the eyes of Collier with a fierce resentment, not of him, but of the fate that had befallen Memphis.

He could not bear that glance. For it showed him suddenly all that he had not been able to guess at in her before this—that she was the true daughter of Jack Memphis. She, too, had her strain of fierce independence, she had her savagery, too. He remembered the first words that he had heard men speak about her.

"You're not here to stay, then?" he asked her. "You're only here until your father's safely out?"

"I'm here forever," she replied tersely. "There's no other place where I feel at home. I know the people, and they know me. I know the country, and the country knows me."

She laughed a little, after she had said this. But then, turning a curious glance on him, she said: "You've held me up and turned me around in your hand to examine me and what I think. What about yourself, Bill Gadsden?"

"Oh, there's nothing much for me to tell you about myself. I'm a pretty dull fellow, and I've lived a pretty dull life."

"A dull life!" she exclaimed.

He felt that he had played the fool. He, the reputed Gadsden, the wild fighter, the long rider, the sharpest knife and the straightest shot in all that country, spoke of the dullness of his existence. No wonder that she was shocked, but there had been such perfect honesty in his voice, and in the emptiness of his far-away look, that she still leaned back a little, staring.

"You've heard of the things they talk about," Collier said. "Well . . . that doesn't mention the dull days, and they're in the majority, by far."

She nodded, and picking up several pebbles, she dropped them one by one.

"I suppose I understand," she said. "I think that Father loves the wild life because of the freedom, and because it's easy to make money, as he says, and because it gives him some authority over other people. But you, Bill, why, you love it the way some men love whiskey!"

He sighed and did not answer, but he turned a dull pink, and knew it by the hotness of his face.

Suddenly her voice was warm with sympathy. "I understand perfectly," she said. "It isn't for the money or even for the fame, or the control of men. It's the simple hunger for danger, danger, danger! That's the red liquor that you want, I see."

She caught her breath as a fuller comprehension dawned upon her.

"Now I know what has drawn you through everything . . . all the wild rides and the gun battles and the knife battles that you've fought, and the wrestling and the fist fights . . . Oh, they've told me a thousand details and stories about you. But do you know that when I first saw you the other night, even though everyone was still gasping because of the way you'd fought Lassiter . . . why, I thought there was something soft and weak and sad about you. Sad, of course. Sad because even a Lassiter didn't really fill your hands."

She tilted a little toward him, and laughed as she laid a hand on his arm.

"I didn't really mean . . . ," he began.

"You didn't mean to be boasting. Of course you didn't," she said. And her laughter was confiding, brooding, inwardly amused. She invited him, as it were, to let her understand his frailty and at the same time promised to deal with it tenderly. "You're red as a little boy ashamed of himself. But it's all right, because I think I understand. The rest . . . they're simply afraid. They've seen you beard the lion and come off without a scratch, but still they're hardly convinced that their eyes have shown them the truth. But I, Bill . . . well, I understand, and I think that I could almost pity you."

"Pity?" Collier repeated, lifting his head at last.

Indeed, he knew that he was an object worthy of pity.

"Because I understand," she said swiftly and softly, "how the love of it must work in you. As the gambler loves racing, and the politician loves speeches, and women love flowers and pretty clothes . . . so you love danger. You risk your life to find your life. There's something half biblical about that, that I didn't intend. But you know, too, that the only thing that gives you joy in the world will one day be the death of you. Ah, but I thought at first it was sheer philanthropy that brought you down to help Father. Now I see that it's simply another great long chance to be exploited. But I wish that I knew some way of filling your mind except with sheer peril."

Her voice, lowered, earnest, rapid, raised in him an echo like the fluttering of a flame in an empty room.

Suddenly he looked at her, straight at her, deeply into her eyes.

"There is one other thing," he said. "One infinitely greater thing, Kate, that would fill my life . . . and if I had it, I could live on a farm and follow the plow all day long."

He stopped, ashamed of himself, for she had suddenly grown scarlet and sat up as straight and stiff as a statue beside him.

XII

He was ashamed of his outburst, for it seemed a taking advantage of her sympathy. She had turned her head quickly away and he lurched to his feet, thoroughly disgusted with himself, prepared to complete that unmasking which already he had contemplated, when it seemed to Collier that he saw a ghost of a smile on her lips.

His purpose was stopped. He was stunned by that discovery. But the broiled trout were now nearly consumed, the coffee was drunk, the pone reduced to a few crumbs, and a crow had flapped down from a branch to pick at a fragment tossed away from the circle.

Collier made a speech, the first of his entire life. It was brief, and tersely pointed. They had come there to discuss ways and means of getting their former chief, Memphis, out of the prison. His daughter was there to help them with her own suggestions. Now let any man who had a thought on the subject come forward with it.

He ended, and he scarcely had finished before a fiery youngster of twenty sprang to his feet like an arrow from a bow.

"We oughta do what Carson done. Charge 'em. He always charged, pop says, when he got into a pinch. I been down and seen the prison. It ain't so easy. But we could wipe out the machine guns easy, with a rush, and then bust open the gate of the prison. We could go down with forty gents ready for trouble and . . ."

The blank face of Collier stopped him. And, as he paused, he looked around and saw the faint smiles of his companions, so that he knew he had been talking rather foolishly. With this, he slumped down to the ground, muttering that no matter how they grinned, his idea was a good one.

"Or let me hear a better one!" he challenged.

Steve Marvin spoke next, and without rising: "We gotta get inside to get Memphis out . . . and him that gets inside is gonna be workin' harder than Memphis deserves."

This speech was a shock to all who heard, though the girl did not change countenance as she listened.

Steve Marvin continued: "It sure ain't easy to stand up before Jack's own girl and talk like this. But I say that Jack was got not fightin' with the crowd, or for 'em. He went down for himself on a private grudge. Lassiter, he sends a challenge, and Jack goes down to meet him. Like a man should go, sure. I admire him fine for goin', too. But when he was dropped, he wasn't fightin' for the rest. Now, I say that the crowd'll go bust if it tries to tangle with the penitentiary. They spent money like water to keep him from gettin' convicted. But he's inside, and he's gotta stay there till his term is up."

He filled his pipe, apparently unconscious of the embarrassed silence around him, and the hot color of the men who acknowledged unwillingly the logic of what he said.

But the girl herself spoke next, sitting at ease, her slim ankles gathered in one hand.

"My father's the last man who would ask

anyone to walk into danger for his sake," she declared quietly. "He wouldn't ask anyone to jump for the moon on account of him. But here you are, all full of cleverness and many devices. Perhaps there's one of them that will hit the target and set him free. There's no harm in talking, if there are any more ideas to circulate. Certainly I don't think we can rush the gate of the prison."

She smiled and nodded at the boy to take the sting out of her last words, and he flushed with pleasure merely to be noticed by her.

However, there were no more comments, no more suggestions. A magpie suddenly commenced to chatter from a nearby tree, and it seemed as though he were pouring contempt and ridicule upon this assembly.

There was a slight but general stir, and all eyes looked with trouble upon the pseudo-Gadsden.

How far was he now from the drowsy afternoons, perched on his stool at the counter of the bank? How far was he now from the heavy-eyed mornings of the little town, and the great oak trees that lined its streets, and the hushing of the sprinklers on all the lawns in the evenings, and the smoke rising from many chimneys, and the sound of many voices, and the whole dreary weight of life where all days wore a single face?

Now, with this clear mountain air of sweetness to breathe, life itself was dearer, and yet the heart grew stronger also. He felt the eyes of these men upon him, but he felt the eyes of the girl still more, resting on him with a silent pressure, a silent demand.

She was expecting from him, what?

Some plan of action, no matter how wild, some rushing into danger so as to fill out the picture that she had conceived of him. He—the danger lover!

He could have laughed, and actually he smiled as he looked down on the others. They were men enough to fight. He at least could be man enough to die, even though he knew the cause in which he struck was already lost.

So in a mood of curious calmness, looking down at them, he looked down at his own petty life and was willing to throw it away.

He told them the plan of Gadsden, word by word. He described what must be done, and how the jailer had been corrupted to make it possible for the prisoner to leave his cell and get into the outer ward of that dark castle of the law. He told of the three machine-gun towers and of how they and their revolving searchlights must be passed—of the guard boats that lay at watch outside the land—of the naked approach to the walls—of the wall itself—and then he took from beneath his coat the slender silken ladder and showed it to them. Quietly he told how the wall must be climbed, the grapnels thrown up, the guards avoided, the prisoner taken to the top of the wall, and then the last desperate sprint for freedom.

He ended.

And, when his voice was still, he saw their fascinated eyes dwelling upon him with a sort of horror. These were men who could walk into a bank in the middle of the day and empty its safe, and shoot their way out to liberty again, and to carouses in the safe mountains. They were men who would not shrink from any single combat. But here they quailed, as he had quailed when the terrible Gadsden outlined the terrors of the task.

It gave him, strangely, an increased power to go on. He raised his voice a little.

"Now, then, my friends," Collier said, "this is the thing to be done, and the only way that I know of in which Jack Memphis can be brought back to you. I think that two men ought to try this thing. Who'll volunteer?"

He waited, and suddenly their eyes fell from his and they exchanged covert glances all around the circle.

The boy stiffened and jerked up his head, but when his lips were already parted for speech, his heart failed him at the grisly prospect. All had been too clearly painted, too logically. And it was the cool morning. Had there been whiskey passed around that circle, half of them would have responded, and having once pledged themselves, not one but would have died gladly rather than falsify his pledged word. But it was the cold, quiet morning, and their sober minds revolted from great peril, and sure death.

Collier filled in part of the pause by saying without emphasis: "I'll make the first one. Which of you will go along with me?"

Again the head of the boy went back, but it dropped, and he sheltered his face in his hands, quivering with eagerness but trembling with dread. He was like a dog baiting a bear.

And still no one answered.

Their glances were on the ground, now, and yet he cruelly maintained the pause, letting them suffer because, with a small-hearted vanity, he wanted the girl to see that what he was attempting, not one of even these chosen men dared to venture upon.

So, when that moment had been prolonged for a while, he made a brief gesture.

"In that case, I'll go alone. How far is it to the prison?"

No one answered still.

Then Steve Marvin growled: "It's thirty mile, at least."

"I'll start now, then," Collier stated. "Will one of you fellows get the horses ready while I pack my roll? I'll need an extra horse for Jack Memphis."

They stood up, every man glad to escape from the cold torment of the girl's watching eyes. They burst away toward the horse shed, except the boy, who lingered for an instant to say: "You can't do it, Bill. Not even you. They'll get you, and no good'll come out of it. You hear? No good'll come out of it! You know that, Bill. You're just gonna throw yourself away!"

The words poured feverishly from him, but Collier shook his head with a smile.

He was anxious to be gone, now, for he felt that it would not take much persuasion to draw him from his task. So his gesture dismissed the lad and sent him stumbling after the others, while Collier slowly turned toward the house.

Kate Memphis stopped him.

"I suppose you did it simply to try them out, but not that you seriously mean that you'll try it?"

"No?" he asked, smiling down at her, somewhat as he had smiled at the others.

"All to make one dull day happy? I tell you," she cried, "it will be merely your last day, Bill!"

"Why, then," he answered, "I'll leave a monument behind me."

"No, no! There'll not even be glory in it. Someone obscurely shot down in the middle of the night. That'll be all. I don't want you to go, not even for my father's sake. Because you're a man, and a king among men, and I won't see you thrown away!"

Some of the truth rose to the lips of Collier against his will.

"If you could know what I am, you'd laugh. And you'd laugh again. But you don't know, Kate. And if they nick me tonight at the prison, you'll never have a chance to guess, even, at the full truth. That's why I'm going."

She went crimson, but endured his steady eye.

"You mean that you go partly for me?"

"All for you. I've never seen your father's face."

"But the men? You've yearned to lead them. Confess that much to me. You've come to take his place with them."

"Would I be going now to get him out, if I were? Suppose it has brought me down here . . . his empty place . . . I'm riding today for you, Kate. Wish me luck!"

He started to move away.

"Will you listen to me for one moment?" she panted, running up beside him. "I want to show you that it's madness, and that . . ."

He waved his hand high in the air. He could even turn his head and laugh over his shoulder at her.

But the knees with which he walked away from her and toward his great adventure were shaking beneath his weight.

XIII

It was almost an utter silence when he left them. Each one muttered good wishes which were barely audible, so greatly did their shame choke them, but still it was not sufficient to make them saddle a horse and ride at his side.

He started up the trail and had almost gained the first bend of the way when he heard the call of the girl behind him and saw her ride out from the trees, but Bud immediately appeared, running after her. He caught the bridle of her horse, and in another moment, Collier was out of sight around the bend.

He wished then with all his heart that she had been free to follow him, for now that his face was set toward the goal, a feather's weight of persuasion would have turned him back. But now she was cut off from him. The bay gelding he rode went eagerly forward, and Lassiter's gray pushed anxiously ahead as far as its lead rope would permit.

Not that he had any hope that two horses, or even one, would be needed for the return trip from the prison, but he had gone ahead mechanically planning the task before him. And now he drifted down through the dark beauty of the woods, finding them more lovely than ever before in all his life. He envied even the chattering squirrels that barked at him from the branches above, and the blue jay that darted like a flung jewel overhead, and the water ouzel that whistled and whirred above the spray of the cataract, for these things lived in happiness which was bounded by no thought of the morrow. And the morning would come up for them bright and clear, while he lay cold, with eyes closed forever. . . .

Sometimes it seemed to him that he was mad to go on, and that he must turn aside from this trail and take any other, he cared not what, so long as it led away. He would fly south or north. He would sell the two fine horses when he came to the railroad. And with the money he would go East, and lose himself there under a new name, among the crowds of some great city.

This was the mind of Collier half the time, and the other half told him that life was short, at the best, flat and pointless, certainly, as he had lived it hitherto. So he would go on, attempt the impossible, and strive to salvage that thousandth chance of which the mocking Gadsden had spoken.

Moreover, he had formed the habit of finishing the task to which he put his hand, a quality useful indeed in the bank, where the back of tomorrow's strength might well be broken by the leftover items from today's program. Habit rules us often where high resolves break down. Habit carried him through now.

He halted twice for a considerable time, for he did not wish to get to the end of his journey much before dark. It was just sunset, in fact, when he came to the verge of the trees and looked out on the last scene.

The spit of land ran into the broken waters of the lake like a long arm, and at the end of it the gray stone walls of the prison stood up like a clenched fist. It held Jack Memphis, who must be rescued from it.

At the shoulder of that arm of land, he could distinguish the machine-gun towers, whose lights were already gleaming pale gold, and beginning to turn, although it was still too early for their illumination to be effective against the last glow of the day. Rows of lights showed in the prison building itself, dull as glowworms in the early evening, and all the lake surface was paved with interchanging purple and gold, and small streaks of uneasy red that twisted here and there.

Never had he seen a place more beautiful, if it had not been for that blunt gray fist appearing in the center, that goal to which he must aspire.

As for the lake itself, as in all things, the description of Gadsden had been perfectly accurate, for he could see three small boats lying at rest, and even now they began to cruise slowly. He saw a puff of white rise at the bows of one, as it lurched through a slapping wave. The nakedness of the spit—which again had been described by Gadsden—was of all things the most depressing.

For it meant a long march toward the machine guns without possible shelter of tree or bush, except that there were numerous hollows, appearing now as spots of deep shadow.

Staring at these, he gained his first dim hope. In this half light, it was possible to cross, not the land, but the lake itself, and to get ashore by swimming to the spit near the prison's outer walls. There he and the horses might lie concealed in one of the deepest hollows until the time for the attempted rescue arrived. If he waited until later, then in the midst of the darkness the searchlights from the guard boats would almost certainly detect two objects as prominent as the heads of horses, and their shoulders battering through the small waves.

He gripped at this hope with a feverish speed and anxiety. When his chances were literally nothing, the least addition to them increased his hope almost infinitely. Suppose, then, that the horses were safely transported to the spit between the machine guns and the prison wall, and suppose that he found there a hollow deep enough to give them a sufficient covert, and suppose, still further, that they did not betray their presence to other watchers by stamping or by neighing—supposing that all these things were true, then surely if once Jack Memphis got over the wall, with two such horses beneath them running at full speed, they would have chances a hundredfold better of bolting past the lights and the guns of the three small watch-towers.

The gold, the red, the purple of the evening had gathered on the lake to the last tone alone, and this was turning darker and duller from moment to moment, when he stripped off his clothes and tied them high on the pommel of the gray. Then he walked down from the trees, leading the horses across the narrow little beach, shivering in the cool cut of the evening breeze.

The light from the nearest guard boat flicked across his eyes as he stepped into the greater cold of the water, but now that he was fairly committed, he would not turn back. He did not believe that anything except eyes of the very greatest power possibly could discern him in this treacherous light between the dark and the day.

The bay horse entered willingly enough, but Lassiter's high-priced thoroughbred reared and snorted—then went forward with a rush that threatened to overturn both Collier and his traded gelding.

However, he managed to straighten out the animals in the water, and once started, it was not difficult to lie between them, helping himself along with one arm and both feet, and keeping the other hand free to guide the animals.

Under the pressure of need, they were docile enough. Each had the heart of a lion, each apparently had grown used to water crossings before this, and, after all, there was only a meager distance to be passed. The water was icy cold, to be sure, but vigorous swimming would mend that.

They bore on very well. The strong exercise, and the fact that at last he had put his hand to the rescue work, both acted on Collier like a strange stimulant, and his heart was higher now than at any time since he left the shack of Bud.

He was halfway across, as he judged, when a more blinding flash of light made him lift himself so as to look over the withers of the bay, and behold, there was the nearest guard ship making straight for him at full speed!

He saw the man standing at her prow, a rifle carried at the ready in his hands. He saw the bright flash of the water as it rose in transparent sheets on either side of the speeding bows, and he told himself that this was the end.

The end before he had well begun.

But what a simpleton he would seem in the eyes of the girl, when she heard of him, taken naked as a fish out of the lake. He had barely crossed the danger line, and here were the dogs of the law to pull him down.

Nearer the boat came. Very distinctly he heard an order given, and with that, she sheered away, and swept off, not fifty feet from him, toward the deeper water.

He was amazed.

He waited for her to come back, but, instead, she circled farther out to the sea, and at last he could understand as he glanced in toward the shore, for all was leaden-colored and dim, in that direction, whereas he had seen the boat up against the last color in the west.

This western light had given the clearness to the craft and the figure on it, but now it had sheered away, and in the shoaling water the feet of Collier touched upon the bottom.

He led the horses up from the lake. It seemed to him that they never would stop rising, that they loomed like giants, and flashed in the sleekness of their wet pelts as though they were afire. Eagerly he dragged at the bits, and slowly, slowly they came after him, still rising loftier, more huge for any eye to see on the higher ground behind the beach. Then suddenly they stumbled down after him into a hollow.

He stood there for a moment gasping with relief. It was a hollow deep enough to cut off most of the force of the wind. It was deep enough, furthermore, to shut him off from all observation. Yet he made as sure of this as he could by creeping up to the top of the nearest sandy crest and scanning the guard boats at sea—none of them stood toward the shore—and the prison walls—from which no men came—and the steadily revolving lights of the machine-gun towers.

But from no side did danger approach.

On that sandy crest he stood up, naked to the wind, and laughed aloud while it pierced his body. For he felt that even should a bullet strike him the next moment, he had done one thing becoming to a man.

Down he went into the hollow, then, and found the two horses close together, heads down, shivering.

It would never do to let them remain like this, and he dared not walk them around until they were dry. So he scooped up handfuls of the dry sand and cast it over them, rubbing them down with all the vigor of his body. It threw him into a glow in spite of his nakedness, and the horses soon had their heads up again under his strenuous efforts.

After that, he dressed himself more leisurely.

For the first time since he had memory, he felt himself a man.

The very horses had changed to him, for they had passed through his hands, and they were his. When he came near them, they nudged him with their muzzles and then looked around with high heads, plainly asking him what his business might be. His heart swelled with possession; it began to grow stronger with confidence, also.

XIV

Midnight struck heavily from the prison bells, the long, deep echoes rolling out across the water.

Collier found that he had fallen almost into a doze, and he roused himself violently. There still remained an hour of waiting before the appointed time, but he felt he must begin to be on the alert. The moon, as Gadsden had prophesied, now stood high in the sky, though there was some faint comfort in the sight of clouds now and then washed across its face and made it seem to dip lower in the heavens, flying back again to a distance as it merged again into the star-sprinkled blackness.

He had induced the horses to lie down, but they had not slept. At least, they were lifting their fine heads to watch him as he approached them now. And when he held out his hand, they sniffed at it in turn, rather like affectionate dogs than horses. He had not known them before, nor any of their kind, but he felt that the pressure of the adventure was drawing them closer and closer together. If he understood them and their valiant loyalty, he felt that they no less understood him and looked to the man's mind to guide them. All this might be imagining but it was an emotion close to the heart of Collier.

He left them behind, more than half afraid that they would whinny after him, but though they jerked their heads around to watch him go, they lay still and made no sound. He went close beneath the walls, keeping to the dark of the hollows as he advanced, until he plainly marked the sentry rounds. There were two men who continually paced back and forth—black forms stepping against the sky—and after meeting and apparently speaking together for a moment, they would turn and pass back to the farthest corners of the outer wall. How he could get a man over that wall under such observance, he could not tell.

He turned to the left, toward the glow of light which indicated the gate through the outer wall, coming quite close to it, before he heard the trampling of a horse nearby. He flattened himself against the ground in the midst of a small swale, and now saw the rider come up to the gate, mounted on a long-legged animal that looked to have every point of quality and speed. Near the gate, the stranger hailed the guards, one of whom came out to him and took an envelope from his hand, disappearing at once, while the newcomer remained in the saddle, walking his horse up and down. At one end of his beat, he came so close to the place where Collier lay that the latter could hear him humming a little song beneath his breath.

It was only a few moments before another man issued in official cap and coat from the lighted gate and, approaching the rider, called out guardedly: "Gadsden! Gadsden! Is that you?"

"Shut up, you dolt!" commanded Gadsden abruptly.

"They can't hear me, and I guess there ain't any ears planted in this ground."

"Nobody's safe till he's inside the front door," Gadsden said. The blood of Collier thrilled as he recognized the voice. "Come here, farther away from that confounded gate, will you?"

They halted not ten steps from the place where Collier lay, now cold with fear lest he should be discovered. Though there was less danger of this now, for a sheeting of thin clouds obscured the moon.

"Buck," said Gadsden, "I've come to give you a chance to step up in your work."

"Yeah, I reckon you have," Buck said sourly. "I come out here when I got your note, but all I gotta say is that I'm through with you, Gadsden. Of all the sneaks, and fish-blooded hounds that I ever knowed, you're the worst."

"Well, well," Gadsden replied without heat,

"you've got your courage up since I saw you last."

"Not a mite," said Buck. "But I know you ain't gonna waste bullets because of words that're spoke to you. It's only when there's an audience around that you're proud. You're a newspaper hero and fightin' man, Gadsden. I know all about you!"

"You're so busy abusing me," Gadsden said patiently, "that you won't listen to the good that I can do for you."

"Good!" sneered the other. "You do good."

"You jackass!" exclaimed Gadsden, at last losing his temper. "I tell you, I can put you in the way of stopping a jailbreak."

"You lie," Buck said. "Or if you don't lie, I don't wanna hear what you have to say to me. You've double-crossed me and made a fool of me too many times before this. I'm through with you and all your kind, Gadsden. Put that in your pipe and smoke it."

"You've gone foolish," Gadsden replied.

"Have I? I've found out the truth from Sally. I've got out of her who told her the facts about me and what I'd done. She throwed me down. And you made her do it with your yapping. Listen to you? If I was ten percent more man, I'd put an end to you."

Gadsden looked away from Buck and up to the sky.

"Will you tell those fellows on the wall to keep their eyes and their ears open?" he asked.

"I'll tell 'em what I please. I've only come down here to tell you that I know what a dog you are . . . to wish you a mean life and a hard death!"

With that, Buck turned his back and walked toward the gate, while Gadsden, after following him for a moment, laughed a little, then called after him: "What you miss will make the sheriff fat, Buck, you idiot!"

He twisted his horse about and galloped back the way he had come, disappearing almost at once among the hollows of the sandy spit.

Collier, sitting up, watched him go with an increasing interest, for he found it difficult in the extreme to follow the course of the fugitive, who dipped out of sight like a fishing bird as it stoops into the trough of the wave, then again his head and shoulders were barely visible, and lost once more. Until finally, near the lights that revolved in the central machine-gun tower, Collier saw him pull up his horse in the full flare of the illumination.

Two things at least he had learned in the last moments. That Gadsden had done his best to betray the plot, and that there was an almost covered way down which a horseman could ride through the center of the peninsula and nearly up to the searchlights.

He turned back toward the walls, hot with

indignation against the traitor, and he found that it was no longer so easy to make out the guards, for every moment the moon grew darker and smaller behind the thickening clouds.

Was there a hope, then, that he could manage to win through to his goal?

On his raised face fell a stinging drop of rain, then a shower rattled upon him, every cold drop striking through to his skin. But after this, began a steady downpour. He lost his pleasure in the darkness, for the stones would now be made slippery, and the climb up the face of the prison wall would be tenfold more difficult.

He did not wait until it was close to one o'clock, but some minutes before he advanced to the foot of the wall and tried the climb. It was as he had expected. The wet shoe leather slid straight off the dripping edges of the stones.

He wrenched off his boots and stockings, and then with his bare feet he attempted the climb again, and found himself mounting at a good rate. Only once his feet slipped completely from beneath him. Jerking down to arm's length, his chin struck heavily against a ledge of masonry, and he felt his fingers slide on the edge of the stonework.

The thrill of terror instinctively made him renew his grip and cleared his head in spite of the stunning blow. He climbed on, and presently he was clinging to the last of the rough masonry.

Above him, his hand found the smooth-sliding wet of the polished stone.

He was very tired. His arms ached fiercely at the shoulders, and his fingers were numb. The cold of the rain penetrated to his spirit, and he would have descended, if it had not seemed that the downward climb was even more blind and perilous than the advance upward.

Peering above him with a cramped neck, he saw a gray form stand in the rain above him, then disappear.

Had Buck, after all, passed on the warning to the guards?

Not through courageous desire to complete his task but from sheer fear of the descent, he tried the ladder, swinging it idly in his grasp for a moment, while his left hand gripped the last ledge to numbness. He could see, now, that it had been an unutterable waste not to have spent every idle moment of the day in practicing the cast of this clumsy line. But at length he gritted his teeth and hurled the irons clumsily upward. Then he flattened himself against the wall with his right hand flung above his head to ward off the falling peril.

It did not fall! He heard a faint but distinct grit of metal points on stone. And when he pulled heavily down on the ladder, it did not give. Here was luck indeed, beyond all price, and at the first throw the ladder was grappled to its place—

though, to be sure, he could not tell how far the grapples were engaged, or if they were about to slip from the wet edge of the stone.

But up the ladder he went. Halfway, and a gust, striking him, swayed him with such violence that he felt for the moment his fall was assured. The rain fell in a palpable weight upon him, but the very force of it seemed to still the wind, and through a pitchy darkness, he gained the top of the wall as the bell of the prison struck one, a mournful note, all whose echoes were lost under the heavy roar of the descending rain. It came so heavily that it stung the back of his hands.

Through it he saw the rays from a few windows—splintered beams of light, and behind him he could trace the wandering arms of the searchlights from the machine-gun towers. On the lake, too, he could spot the guard boats, cruising back and forth, close in shore.

Gathering up the rope, he flung it down into the outer ward of the prison, whose paved floor looked like dimly glimmering water in the distance. There was no sign of Jack Memphis in that yard.

He determined that he would wait five minutes, and then retreat, when without warning, either of sight or sound, a man's body toppled over him from the side, and he rolled with the unknown to the verge of the prison wall. His head and shoulders hung over a great abyss of rain-filled emptiness!

XV

He could have been cast over the edge easily, but the man who had blundered into him was as apparently taken by surprise as he, and was unprepared to meet the desperate struggle which he put forth immediately. It whirled his assailant over. Collier saw a contorted face gasping and cursing up at him. He needed merely to draw a revolver from the guard's holster in order to make the day his. With the muzzle of the gun pressing under his chin, the man lay still, frightened white, as Collier could see in spite of the dark of that rainy night.

He tied the guard with strips from the man's own clothes, and wedged a handkerchief between his teeth to assure his silence.

Then he turned back to the silken ladder.

Already the grapples were being jerked at, and the cords were stirring, but he could not see into the dark, which now was filled with a dense rain mist, thick as heavy dust. Then, out of that mist, up swayed the head and shoulders of a man who now gripped the wall edge, accepted the extended hand of Collier, and stood erect on the top of the wall.

He peered once at Collier, muttering: "I thought it was gonna be Gadsden." Then he gathered up the ladder and flung it down on the outside of the wall.

He waved to Collier to precede him, but the latter insisted: "They've got more against you than against me, Memphis!"

There was no argument. Down the ladder went Jack Memphis, and the younger man behind him. At the bottom, they let the ladder hang behind them without delaying to try to throw the grapples from their hold. And Collier stumbled forward through the sand toward the hollow where he had left the horses.

The animals were on their feet, and though they lurched back from the rush of the men, they were instantly captured and the two swung up into the saddles.

"Which way?" cried Memphis.

The boom and then the rapid jangle of an alarm bell began to strike from the prison interior, and the gray horse, on which Memphis was mounted, snorted and stamped at the angry sound.

"Whichever way, the quickest one is best for us," Collier declared. "Come with me!"

And he headed the bay gelding straight up the sand spit along the course which he had seen Gadsden take earlier in the evening. From a hummock top they looked back and saw the gates of the prison spouting out armed men, whose weapons glistened faintly in the rain. And then as a shaft of light from the machine-gun towers cut across them, they dropped into safe darkness again, and shot out on the farther side close under the last line of danger.

Collier saw the light flash brightly upon the broad-striped suit of prison clothes which his companion wore, and as he saw the clearness with which they stood out in the night, he was struck with fear again. As a red flag could be seen in the bright rays of the sun, so would these bars show in the lighted rainstorm.

They were plunging straight toward the center tower with its swinging pair of lights, and big Memphis, swaying out in the saddle, shouted: "A gun, kid! A gun!"

Into his hand, Collier pressed the weapon which he had taken from the guard, and instantly it flashed three times as Memphis fired at the two shadowy forms within the central tower. One of them lurched aside and went down. The chatter of the machine gun ceased. Then, as the fallen figure rose again, the weapon began to pour out bullets after them, and Collier knew, with a strange sense of relief, that the guard could not have been badly hurt.

Three streams of bullets rattled now through the brush about them. From each of the towers was raining its own stream after them, but the rain was a thick mantle through which the search-lights broke only partially, and the brush itself now began to sweep over them in shrouding shadows, when big Jack Memphis half turned in the saddle and pointed behind him.

"They're after us, and after us hard, son!"

It was difficult for Collier to look back. His mind was fully occupied with keeping in the wet saddle at the terrific pace which the bay gelding maintained, but, risking a glance, he saw far behind him, dimly illumined by the last touch of the searchlights from the towers, a single rider reaching after them through the rainstorm with all the speed of a magnificent horse.

They passed through a narrow screen of trees, now, and coming onto the open road, Memphis swung the gray to the right. They began to make terrific pace up the easy going, for the road was sand and gravel, which held perfectly in spite of the rain.

Sometimes they passed through a runlet of water that crashed up against the chests and the flying knees of the horses, but they went on with unabated speed for some minutes, until the horses of their own volition came back a little on the bits.

Memphis did not urge them forward, and Collier breathed a great gasp of relief. For he felt that the shaking he was receiving between pommel and cantle could not be endured much longer. It was as though he rattled in every joint.

Jack Memphis, dropping the reins, threw out

his arms and, tossing back his head, he let the fast-falling rain beat against his face.

"Free, by gosh!" he shouted. "Free, kid, and never meant for the inside of walls again."

He rode on at a jog trot, still laughing, still exulting, while a changing wind, that perhaps had brought up this last clearing shower, now cuffed the clouds aside and let the moon shine through.

For the first time, Collier could see the father of Kate Memphis, and he saw a rugged man in the prime of life with an eye that even the rain-dimmed moon shine could not make dull.

"I thought it was Gadsden coming!" he said. "Who are you, kid? And here's Jack Memphis's hand, no matter how long or short he lives. To the end of him, kid, he's all with you."

It was impossible to lie to this man. The whole story came briefly to the lips of Collier.

"I'm Hugh Collier. I'm a bank clerk on a vacation, but I ran into Gadsden, and he traded this bay for the nag I was riding. When I got to town, I was taken for the real Gadsden because of the scar on my face . . . you can't see it by this light. Lassiter came and jumped me . . . I managed to break away from him and get his gun. . . ."

"You managed that?"

"I'm no man-killer, Memphis. It was luck . . . and being scared like a cornered rat. Bud took me away to his shack. That night Gadsden slipped

126

in and told me I'd better ride off, but somehow I liked the part I'd been playing in this game, and I wanted to stay. He told me the plan to set you free, and because he owed me something for what I'd done in taking Lassiter off his trail, he said that I could try to work the thing through. So here I am, as you see."

"Owed you enough to let you risk your neck, eh? That's a pretty good kind of a debt to have. I wish I had a dozen of 'em!"

"It's finished," Collier said, with a half sigh. "But who's that coming behind us?"

They heard the stroke of a long-striding horse at full gallop, and, looking back, they saw two riders rounding the curve behind them.

"Lassiter, Lassiter!" shouted Memphis. "Him ridin' aslant . . . I'd know his style. They're after us, son. He's for me, and you take the gent on his right. Lassiter, by gravy, and I'll cross off that score tonight!"

They swept on closer beneath the moon, and Collier saw that the face of Lassiter was like that of a mummy, so swathed was it with bandages to the eyes.

But for his own part he faced whom? Gadsden, beyond a doubt! Gadsden, the treacherous, but Gadsden, the terrible! Gadsden the deceitful, the cunning, the man of fox-like wiles!

He drew his revolver—the same that he had taken from Lassiter—and gripped it hard. All his life fear had been his companion at every crisis, but now as he looked back to the thought of the high, rain-polished wall, and the circling lights, and the hushed danger of the long sand spit extending into the lake, it seemed to him that this was nothing whatever.

And with a great rush of blind anger, he watched them drawing rein, the two, and saw them whip out flashing weapons. Let them pause for sure aim. He, who had no skill, would not wait.

He drove his heels into the sides of the bay gelding, and as it pitched heavily forward into a run, half stumbling as it fought to gain headway on the slippery road, he began firing. As he fired, and the handle of the weapon kicked back strongly against the heel of his hand, wild joy sprang up in the heart of Collier. He shouted, although he knew not that he was shouting. His throat strained with the piercing yell that tore through his lips.

So he charged in, and saw Gadsden, at first erect, then drop lower, and shoot with stiffly extended arm, like one who is striving to push an ardent danger away from close range.

Suddenly he lurched lower still. His left arm clung about the neck of his horse for an instant, but as the frightened beast shied violently away, Gadsden fell heavily to the ground and lay there on his back with his arms thrown wide, just as the sheriff went down, horse and man, beneath the bullets of Memphis.

Collier, his exultation snuffed out like a flame, swung down to the ground, and knelt beside the wounded man. He saw that Memphis already was busy extricating the fallen sheriff from the tangle.

Pale and still lay Gadsden under the moon— dead, thought Collier—dead by the spreading dark stain upon his breast, and he, Collier, had slain this man!

But here the eyes of Gadsden opened suddenly. He coughed, half strangled, and then with one wild glance around him, he knew where he was and what had happened to him. He nodded at Collier.

"Beginner's luck, kid," he said.

"Are you badly hurt?" breathed Collier. "What can I do?"

"Stop worrying," Gadsden said. "I've got my share, but only that I've played a double game for a long time, always inside the law, and always seeming outside of it. Not even Lassiter knew that I was on the inside, till tonight. I thought I had a trap framed that would catch the rest of Memphis's gang . . . but I've only caught myself, and they'll never hang you for this. I've got too many counts against me, as they'll find when they begin to read a little deeper in my case. Collier, I'm going out. Shake hands before I finish."

It was his left hand that he extended, but Collier, amazed and startled by what he had heard, accepted that hand.

Suddenly he was jerked closer. A knife flashed in the other hand of Gadsden. A fraction of a second sooner, and he would have had the strength to drive it home, but as it was, the weapon turned sidewise, and only his fist struck feebly over Collier's heart. Then Gadsden fell limply back, and stirred no more.

XVI

Now Collier heard Jack Memphis speaking close beside him. He saw the sheriff remounted, but this time on the horse of the dead man. And with bowed head, Lassiter gripped the pommel of the saddle.

"You'll get to the prison soon enough for them to fix you up," Memphis was saying, "and when that happens, you'll be able to take a rest pretty nigh as long as you need. When you lay there, spell the thing out for yourself. Ask yourself if huntin' men ain't worse than what I do, which is huntin' money. So long, Lassiter. Here's hopin' that there ain't no third meetin' between us."

In a half trance, the boy watched the sheriff ride off down the road, first at a walk, and then at a trot. The voice of Memphis broke in at his side.

"Leave Gadsden lay here," he said. "Lassiter will send back for him. We gotta get on. But what'll this mean to you?"

"Nothing, I suppose," said Collier. "I don't think Gadsden has had enough time to tell Lassiter who I am. I think there may have been enough shame in him to keep him from that. And so no one knows Hugh Collier. I can fade out of the picture."

"What was in Gadsden? Was he crazy?"

"I don't know. I suppose he was one of those danger lovers, that I've heard people talk about. Poor Gadsden. He wanted to be on both sides of the fence, and now he's dead, and heaven forgive him."

They mounted and turned back up the road.

They made no haste in that progress, but jogged the horses slowly forward, stopping to make supper, before daybreak, on some provisions which were in Collier's saddlebags for that purpose. And it was the brightest and most colorful moment of the morning when Kate Memphis found them rounding a curve on the upper trail.

Collier was a few lengths behind, at the moment, and he drew rein to watch her throw up her hand, and then to see her lost in the arms of her father. It came to him with a sense of wonder, like a thing read in a book, that it was he who had done this miracle and had brought the man home to her. He waited with a foolish smile, half in dread of the moment when she should notice him.

But when that moment came, she was wonderfully cold and casual. It was merely a cheerful good morning, and no more—no melting of the eyes, no trembling of the voice, nothing to show that she was more than politely grateful to this unhired deliverer.

He gritted his teeth. He was shamed by the very height of his expectations.

The rose left the morning, the sun was growing warm, the birds had ceased from the first ecstasy of their singing, and the eyes of Collier fell down to the rutted road, watching the sinuous trails which had been cut in the surface, and the little trickles of water which ran here and there across its surface.

His heart was down lower than the pavement, for he had been listening to the bubble and the flow of the girl's voice as she chattered merrily with her father.

Suddenly, Memphis waved her ahead. "I'm going up to the camp alone, to give the boys a surprise," he said, "but before I start, I gotta say something to the kid, here." He reined back to Collier and spoke to him aside.

"Son," he said, "you don't look none too happy."

"I'm happy enough," Collier said.

"You look it!" said the other ironically. "Tell me, son, if I'm a liar, or was it Kate, that you had in your eye when you rode down there to swim lakes and climb walls and gag guards and shoot Gadsdens . . . the crooked, double-crossin' swine! Was it Kate that you had in your mind?"

Collier flushed. "Certainly not," he said.

The big man laughed. "I wouldn't grudge her to you," he said. "She's too good for the sort of a life that she'd find with the mountain men. She's been raised for something better and a damned sight softer. She belongs to your kind of a man, my lad."

Collier sighed, but did not answer.

"You think that she's forgot what you've done, eh?" said the other. "You listened to her chatter, but you didn't see when she sneaked glances at you, now and then, like a sick calf. Now, mind you, I'm gonna go up the road to the camp, and after I'm gone, you wait here a minute, as though you and her had to give me time clearance to get clean away. But when you're alone with her, if you're half the man that I figure on you to be, you'll sure make her see things your way.

"Mind you, she's got a stubborn streak. Take her, son, because there's nobody else in her mind except you. Take her, and snake her along with you back to that town you was telling me about. It'll be me that'll give you a flying business

133

start, but if you don't take her away from the mountains, if you settle with her up here, what kind of a life would you have except a wild life, and what would your children be except wild kids?"

Young Collier raised his head and looked about him. He was sad in spite of the new hope that was born in him, but still as he thought of the drab little town, and then looked about on the lofty trees, and the noble mountains, and heard the voice of the water and the voice of the wind, he could not help sighing at the thought of making an exchange.

The outlaw said no more, but, putting the Lassiter gray to a gallop, he rode strongly around the first curve and then the second.

There he stopped. He never had intended to ride straight on to the camp, as he declared. He merely dismounted here and walked nervously from one side of the road to the other, while he smoked one pipe after another.

And, as he walked up and down, he tried to build for himself the life that would be his when the girl was away from him in the lowlands, but his imagination failed in the effort.

At last, he flung himself back into the saddle and turned the horse about. Through the trees by a straight cut he reached the side of the road again, and then slipping the horse forward gradually, he peered out through the last screen of shrubbery and saw the two. No matter what fear and doubt had possessed the boy, it had been conquered.

He was beside the girl, their two horses rubbing shoulders, going lazily forward, softly, in step with one another, and keeping a course as foolishly meandering as a wagon wheel's trace on the highway.

They did not talk. But they laughed, as only young fools can, and worshiped one another.

It was not this, however, which filled the heart of the father with the last scruple of pleasure, but the fact that they were riding not down to the safe country, the law-abiding, but, though slowly, toward the wild and happy highlands where he, Jack Memphis, was king.

At that, secretly and softly he drew back the gray, and when he had gotten to a safe distance, galloped the horse bravely up the road, laughing as he went.

The Magic Gun

I

On Saturday night at eight o'clock, or a very little after, Lewis Dikkon looked up from mellowing some lifts and top pieces for heels, and saw a stranger in the doorway.

"Do you want something?" Dikkon asked, putting the little tub of water to one side.

"I want a seat," said the stranger.

Dikkon waved to the two chairs that stood against the wall. The stranger took one of these, but he placed it so that it faced the open door, before he sat down. In this manner little more than his profile was turned to Dikkon, who saw a lean and brown face and a sharp, blue eye with a maze of wrinkles at the corner.

It was not unusual for people to come in, in this fashion. Sometimes a cowpuncher would sit for hours watching the fashioning of the boots which were one of his few luxuries.

Outside on the street, Dikkon was not greatly respected, because his pale face showed that he lived indoors, but in the shop he was rather looked up to. This stranger, however, paid little attention to the boot-making. He preferred to sit and stare through the dark at the opposite side of the square and the trees which dotted it.

"It's quiet, here," said the stranger after half an hour or so.

This was the only explanation which he vouchsafed. For a whole hour he remained in that chair. Then he rose, replaced it against the wall, and left with a curt good night.

Dikkon thought no more of him until, at just the same hour the next Saturday, the same man appeared. He merely nodded at Dikkon and took the place that he had occupied the week before. Only, on this occasion, he did not spend all his time staring through the doorway across the square. He favored Dikkon with an occasional glance.

"Pretty good pay?" he asked after a long silence.

"Yes," Dikkon answered, "I get five dollars a week."

The stranger exclaimed: "Five dollars! Is that good pay? Why, even an ornery puncher like me gets many times that."

"Look what you gotta do," Dikkon pointed out. "You gotta ride in all kinds of weather, hot and cold. All I do is sit still. I got a roof over my head all the time."

"All you gotta do is sit still?" said the cow-puncher. "Ain't that hard enough?"

He gave an odd effect, as though he were always appealing to a third person when he spoke, because he never looked back at Dikkon except in swift, bright flashes. The rest of the time he was staring through the door.

"Hard?" Dikkon echoed, not able to understand.

"Don't you get numb?" asked the cowpuncher.

"The first few years. Not after that. I got used to it."

No more was said. An hour slipped away. The puncher rose and nodded good night and was gone.

Another week followed, and at eight o'clock on Saturday night the cowpuncher came in and resumed his place. He seemed to feel the half-startled curiosity in Dikkon's eyes for, though he would not turn his head from the door and what lay beyond it, he explained: "You got the quietest place in town. I get dog-goned tired of the rattle of the voices and the foolishness down where they're blotting up the red-eye. I don't bother you none, my sitting here?"

"Not a bit," Dikkon said. "I like to have you. It's a sort of company."

"Thanks," said the puncher.

For a half hour he was silent, and Dikkon sighed. It was not often that he had such a chance for conversation, and now it was wasted.

As though his thought had been divined, the stranger said suddenly: "You don't talk much, kid."

"You get in the habit of listening, not talking, sitting here like this," said Dikkon.

141

"Yeah. I'd guess that. How long you been doin' it?"

"Fifteen years, about."

"Hey. That's long enough. How old are you?"

"Twenty-two."

"You started at seven?"

"My uncle says that nobody is too young to work at shoes."

"You work for your uncle, eh?"

"Yes."

"For five a week?"

"Yes. He's been paying me ever since I was eighteen."

"You worked eleven years, first?"

"You gotta put in apprentice time," explained Dikkon.

The cowpuncher did not answer. He took out a plug of black chewing tobacco, brushed off some straw which stuck to it, and then worked off a chew. This he stowed in his cheek where it made a mound with a white top—like a little model of a mountain.

"That's two fifty a year," said the puncher.

"It ain't all cash," admitted Dikkon. "I get two a week in cash. The rest goes back into the business."

"It does!"

"That way, I'll have a half interest when I'm thirty."

"That's twelve years at a hundred and fifty.

Add on some interest. It's over two thousand dollars. Is this here shop worth four thousand and something, kid?"

Dikkon stopped to consider. He fell into a brown study, and when he looked up from it with an answer, the stranger was gone.

But the next week, punctually, he returned to his chair. On this occasion he sat out the entire hour without saying a single word. But as he was leaving, he turned and leaned in the doorway.

"Well, what about it?" he asked.

Dikkon knew what he meant and he admitted: "No, I don't suppose this place is worth four thousand . . . quite."

"Your uncle owns the land?"

"No, he rents that."

"Well, five hundred dollars' worth of shack. That's too high, though. A hundred iron men for tools. A hundred for leather and such. You could buy out this dog-goned job for a thousand, kid. You buckle onto that!"

Dikkon thought of it for a week, turning the facts slowly in his mind. He was not a fool; he simply had been kept in a small pasture and had not learned to jump obstacles as he met them. He was sewing on soles when the stranger came, as usual, at eight o'clock on Saturday night.

He took his chair, and presently he remarked with irritation: "There's a lot of wind and dust tonight!"

"Does it blow in on you?" asked Dikkon.

"No, but you can't hardly see across the square."

He bit his lips and seemed half nervous and half angered. Presently he began to notice Dikkon again, with his usual side glances.

"You always stay open at night?"

"Yes. Uncle Charles takes Monday, Wednesday and Friday. I take the other nights."

"How late?"

"Ten."

"When you begin?"

"Six."

"That's sixteen hours," said the puncher.

"It comes to about that."

Half an hour went by. Suddenly the stranger said: "How come you don't get a hump on your back, sitting all day like that?"

"I don't know," Dikkon answered slowly. "I never thought of that."

"Humph!" said the stranger.

At the end of his hour—he was never a single minute past nine in leaving—he paused an instant.

"Gimme that leather and the awl," he said.

When he had it, he worked the awl slowly through the sole. Then he handed it back to Dikkon.

"You got fingers of iron," he said. "Do any shooting?"

"Not much," said Dikkon.

"You'd have a steady hand," observed the cowpuncher, and departed.

Those weekly visits began to be oases of pleasure in the desert of the boy's life, and yet he rather dreaded them. He had been greatly upset by the cowpuncher's valuation of the shop, for he did not like to think that his uncle was cheating him on such a gross scale. However, the seed of doubt was sowed and it soon sprang into flower.

There was another shoemaker down the street, and Dikkon visited him during the Wednesday noon hour. He was well received. Yonder shoemaker was a wide-shouldered little Italian with a bowed back.

"Suppose," Dikkon said hesitantly, "that I wanted a job?"

Light flashed into the eyes of the other.

"I'd take you quick enough," he said.

"How?"

"Say fifteen a week."

Dikkon grew blank.

"I mean," hastily corrected the Italian, "I'd start you in at fifteen. I'd boost you pretty quick."

Dikkon went out into the sun with thoughts spinning rapidly through his brain.

Five dollars a week—two dollars down!

On his way back, he met their landlord, and stopped him.

"Suppose that we wanted to sell the shop," he asked. "What could we get?"

"I dunno," said the landlord. "Say, five or six hundred?" He shrugged his shoulders when he saw Dikkon agape.

"I ain't offering to buy it," he declared, and passed on rudely without another word.

So Dikkon went back to the shop, and, laying his hands on the counter, he looked down at the face of his uncle. Mr. Bender's chin and forehead sloped sharply back, yet no one could say that his was a weak face. With his long nose and bright little eyes, he looked like a rat.

"Well, well," snapped Charles Bender. "Are you a customer? Come in here! Look what you done to the waist of that boot. Look at it, I say! Master worker? Master fool!"

Dikkon went in and sat down. He made no response. He had learned to listen and to think in the past fifteen years, and now he had something to think about.

II

For two hours he worked, and then he said: "Uncle Charles . . ."

"Chatter, chatter, chatter!" said that irritable and silent man. "Now what you want?"

"Money!" said young Dikkon.

"Money, eh?" growled Bender. "Well, I want money, too!"

For another hour Dikkon worked without a word. Then he said again: "Uncle Charles."

"You oughta be a minstrel," Uncle Charles commented. "Always yappin'. Now what you want?"

"Money," Dikkon announced.

He was aware, without looking to the side, that his partner on the bench had flashed a keen glance at him from beneath those hanging, shaggy brows, like the brows of an old rat.

"You wanna new suit, eh?" the uncle asked more mildly. "One of these days you're gonna have it. One of these days."

"I don't want a new suit," Dikkon said.

"That's good," murmured Uncle Charles, and deliberately filled his mouth with nails.

Dikkon saw that this was meant to preclude all conversation, but he had advanced so far that he had gained great impetus, and could not stop himself.

"I want a gun!" he blurted.

The nails descended in a shining shower. Only part of them were caught by the claw-like hand of Charles Bender. The rest splashed to the floor.

"Look what you made me do!" Bender said rather childishly. "Now you get down and pick 'em all up, and don't you miss none."

Dikkon got down on hands and knees and

gathered the nails and restored them to the hand of his uncle. He climbed back onto the bench and sat down. For another hour he worked rapidly, steadily. But only half of his mind was in his work. Long ago he had learned this business so well that half of his wits could be wandering in distant lands.

"Uncle Charles," he began again.

"Yes, yes, yes!" snarled the little man, and he writhed. "Lemme be, will you?"

"I want some money," said Dikkon. "I want to buy a gun."

"Why on earth do you hound me?" Uncle Charles shouted, red with fury. "You got money, ain't you? What you want with a gun? What could you do with a gun? What good would it be to you?"

"I got a steady hand for a gun," said the boy.

He held out the heavy heeling hammer. It lay straight without a quiver, never stirring in the tips of his fingers. The big cords of the wrist stood out like drawn wires under the continued strain, but still the hammer did not quiver.

"You got a steady hand, have you?" asked the other. "Then you go and buy yourself a gun, if you want to. If you're gonna be a fool, don't come to me for advice . . . or money!"

He spoke with such bitter violence that the boy said no more. There was no hurry. He had lived for fifteen years in this manner. Now he would

148

think a little longer before he took a step that brought down danger on his head.

The next morning, also, he still delayed. There was time. He waited until the bright warmth of prime.

"Uncle Charles," he said.

"What's the matter with you?" barked the other.

"Speaking about that money . . ."

"I never heard nothing like you," Charles Bender declared. "You been ravin' at me about money for a week. You don't let me have no peace! You want money? You got money. Or you ought to have it!"

"I don't think so," Dikkon said.

"You don't think what? Don't think I ain't been payin' you hard cash money every week here for years and years? I seen a time," Uncle Charles reflected sadly, "when a young man, he didn't dare to ask for a penny until he got to be twenty-five. He knew that he was just a fool boy till then. But you've been hangin' around the street corners, and you been pickin' up all sorts of ideas."

"I don't hang around the street corners," Dikkon said.

"I've seen you! I've seen you!" Uncle Charles pointed a scrawny finger.

"I don't hang around the street corners," Dikkon went on, "because the people stare at me."

"Because they know you'd ought to be home, doin' chores, or sittin' here on this bench, learnin' to be a man!"

"Because my clothes are funny. That's why they point at me."

"It's a lie!" Bender cried savagely.

"It ain't a lie. I've looked. I know. I feel chilly in the back whenever I go outside."

"You're a fool, then. What's wrong with your clothes? You got a coat and hat and trousers and shoes."

"Look!" Dikkon said.

He held out his arms. His sleeves crawled halfway to his elbows.

"That's why they look at me funny," said Dikkon.

That fact seemed so clearly apparent that even Uncle Charles could not argue the point further. He merely squealed in a passion: "Who you been talkin' to? Who's been puttin' these ideas into your head? Eh? Eh? Eh?"

He caught the arm of Dikkon and shook it. His hands were not as strong as Dikkon's, but, nevertheless, the fingers were sharp enough to bite to the bone.

"Don't do that," Dikkon said, jerking his arm. "You don't hurt me and you don't frighten me."

Uncle Charles removed his hand with a grunt. "Sulky, ain't you?" he asked.

But his voice had altered, and there was something like fear in his eyes.

"You think you're a man, don't you?" he suggested almost mildly.

"You never frightened me," said Dikkon. "Not even when I was little. You used to hurt me, then, but you never frightened me. Are you going to listen?"

"What have you got to ask me?" demanded Bender.

"I want money."

"Aye, and I've heard you say that before. Ain't I been paying you out good money? Why not use that? Are you a miser?"

"You've given me," the boy said, "four hundred dollars in fifteen years."

"I've given you that, have I?" gasped the shoemaker, choking with anger. "What about the sums that I been layin' into the business for you?"

"What's this place worth?" Dikkon asked.

"Thousands! Why do you ask?"

"You try to sell it," Dikkon said. "They'll give you five hundred for the shop. That's all."

Bender leaned far back and tipped up his head. He began to laugh, but he was so excited that his lips furled back over his teeth and he merely panted, making no sound of mirth. He looked more like a rat than ever, like a poisoned, frenzied rat.

Dikkon regarded him calmly. He had known of this similarity before, but he never had known it so dearly.

"Five hundred! Five thousand, you young fool!"

"You go and find out," Dikkon suggested. "Ask Mister Jackson."

That was the landlord.

"What'd he say?" the shoemaker demanded savagely. "Five hundred?"

"He wouldn't pay that."

"He wouldn't! He . . . he . . ."

"You want me to work eight more years. Take three dollars out of every week's wages . . . that's more than two thousand dollars, counting interest."

Bender clasped his hands together and held them hard.

"You're that kind of a man, are you?" he asked. "That's the sort of viper you are, are you? Thinkin' meanness! Layin' up unkindness!"

"It really is a lot more than that. My wages ought to be more than five dollars a week."

"Ought they? You been doin' what? What you think you ought to be gettin'?"

"Fifteen a week."

Uncle Charles laid his head back on his shoulders and looked at the ceiling again as if he were under a greater burden than he could bear.

"Go on!" he gasped.

"In twelve years, at thirteen dollars a week. That's a good deal. Let's see. That's nearly eight thousand dollars, just about. More, with interest!"

Uncle Charles leaped to his feet. "You're crazy!" he shouted.

Dikkon defiantly put aside his work and folded his hands. He felt calmer the angrier the other grew. It always had been that way with him, even in the first dreadful years, when the torture was newly biting into his flesh and into his heart and soul.

"I don't think so," he said.

"Eight thousand dollars!" the shoemaker shouted. "I . . . I could buy a hundred like you, for that!"

"Why do you think so?"

"Don't I know men?"

"I suppose you do," Dikkon said. "You know prices, anyway. You never charge a low rate."

"I get good money because I do good work."

"Yes, it is good," admitted Dikkon.

"I do the best work in the town or the county."

"More than half of your work is mine," Dikkon reminded him.

It seemed like a blow with a fist to the little man. He actually shrank away until his narrow, rounded back thumped against the rear of the counter.

"More than half . . . ," he began.

"Ever since I was fourteen or fifteen," Dikkon

153

continued, "I've done more work than you do. And since I was eighteen or nineteen, I've done better work. I make all the best boots. I've made them all for three years."

"Gratitude!" Uncle Charles shouted. "That's gratitude. Because I been givin' you the pleasant work, the work that's pretty, tryin' to make a master shoemaker out of you . . . by Jiminy, I'm gonna fire you right now. You get out!"

"I will," Dikkon said. "I can go down the street to Fanchetti's. He'll pay me fifteen a week . . . and boost me right up, afterward!"

III

Immediately he was sorry that he had spoken in such a manner. He was almost frightened by the look of greed, rage, fear, and cunning malice that convulsed the face of Charles Bender. The latter snatched up a hat and rushed out into the open, forgetting that he still had on his working apron.

Dikkon picked up his tools and laid them neatly away. He was putting on his own hat when his uncle returned.

"What are you doin'?" the latter asked.

"You told me to go."

His uncle took him by the shoulders and pushed him into a chair.

"You don't think that I meant it?" he asked. He

began to laugh and rub his hands together. "Why, Dikkon, ain't I your uncle? Ain't I your flesh and your blood?"

"I suppose you are," Dikkon admitted gravely.

"You go back there and sit down on the bench. You want a gun. Why, Dikkon, don't I love you? Would I stint you? No, I wouldn't. I'll give you a gun. I got an old rifle up in my room. It's as good as new."

"It hasn't any lock," Dikkon said.

"I can get a new one, though."

But Dikkon thought back to the man who first had put all these notions in his mind. He remembered the two guns that swung low on his thighs.

"I want a Colt," he said.

The uncle blinked.

"I know Eastman that keeps the second-hand shop. He'll get one better than new for you. You leave it to me."

But Dikkon could not help looking back to other purchases that his uncle had made for him. Always he did the shopping. And always he brought him odd-looking garments at a strangely high price.

"I want to buy my own gun," he said.

"Well, well, well. Go back and sit on the bench. What's today?"

"Monday . . . Tuesday, I think."

"Scatter-brained child you are. Don't even

know the day of the week. I'll see if I can rake up some money for you before the end of the week. I . . . I'll borrow you five dollars, maybe. Blindheim, the moneylender. Maybe he'll lend it to me."

"I was just thinking of something else," Dikkon said.

"You're doin' a lot of thinkin' lately," Uncle Charles said with the gloomy shadow rushing back across his face.

"I was wondering why we're so poor," Dikkon said.

"Why? Because fate made us that way!"

"How do you spend your money, then?" asked Dikkon.

"Ha!" cried the older man, turning pale.

"I know what you make," Dikkon continued. "You make a lot. You have the highest prices, and you have all the work you can do. We don't spend anything. We have meat once a week. A new suit once in four years . . . and that's second-hand. Well, then, where does the money go?"

Bender drew a great breath, and Dikkon saw that his forehead, indeed his whole face, was drawn with anger.

"I know," Dikkon went on, "that you've cleared a terrible lot every week. You've never had any hard times. Not since I've been with you. Lately, you've made more than a hundred dollars a week . . . all clear. That's . . ."

"That's a lie!" shouted the uncle.

"The cash book blew open on the floor. I saw it," Dikkon informed him.

"You've been spyin'!" Uncle Charles yelled.

"That's five thousand a year," Dikkon went on. "That's fifty thousand in ten years. There's interest piling up, too. You must have a hundred thousand or so laid away and . . ."

"No, no, no!" Uncle Charles wailed.

"And now I want enough to buy a Colt . . . a good Colt!" Dikkon kept going on. "Or else you can get a new man to work in here on the bench."

"You're g-going to have it," Uncle Charles stammered. "Ain't I said that you're gonna have it? Next week . . ."

"Tomorrow by noon," Dikkon stated.

The other blinked and writhed. "Tomorrow by noon," he finally admitted.

"Well, then, I'll go back to work. But I have to have ammunition, too."

This was received in silence, after which, as Dikkon seated himself on the bench, a soothing hand fell on his arm and stroked it.

"I'm gonna do everything for you, Dikkon," the miser said. "I'm gonna make you a happy boy, someday. You ask what I got? Well, I got something put away, sure enough. And who does it go to? Who does it go to? Don't I have to die, someday?" He shuddered as he said it.

"Only," he went on, "you be a good boy and tell me . . . was it Fanchetti that put these here ideas into your head?"

Dikkon looked up and shook his head.

"Who was it, then?"

"I thought them out myself . . . almost all," Dikkon answered.

Uncle Charles, with a heavily working face, lingered a moment, as though about to take his seat on the bench beside his neighbor, but presently he sighed and murmured that he was sick and would have to lie down for a while. So through the rear door he went, tottering.

Afterward, Dikkon heard steps of diminishing sound when the door was closed, but he knew that his uncle had not moved on down the hall. He was crouched there, looking through the wide, worn keyhole and trying to spy out some secret on Dikkon's features.

But the boy worked on, never raising his face for fear that the triumph that he felt should appear in his eyes.

Finally he detected a stealthy sound in the distance, as Uncle Charles at last went softly up the stairs. And Dikkon sighed with relief.

The next day he waited for his money, but it was not forthcoming. It was not even mentioned, and the day following there was a brief explanation that the bank had done something wrong, and it would take a few days to arrange matters.

Dikkon guessed that this was a lie, but he did not want to use sterner measures. He felt that on the occasion of the first encounter he had taken his uncle in the palm of his hand and broken down all his defenses. Now he could take the advantage whenever he chose, but he would not hurry.

Then Saturday came, and he began to look forward with a growing excitement to the coming of the stranger.

The latter, sure enough, came punctually into the shop and took up his accustomed place without more than a nod of greeting. But it seemed to Dikkon that he had a thousand things to say, and the hour that stretched before him was all too short a time.

"You've never told me your name?" he suggested suddenly.

The stranger flashed him the usual side glance.

"You've never told me yours, kid."

"I'm Lewis Dikkon."

"That's a queer name . . . Dikkon."

"And yours?" Dikkon persisted.

"Well," said the other, "I'm Sam Prentiss, I suppose."

It seemed odd to Dikkon that a name should be stated in such a manner.

Presently Prentiss murmured: "You been eatin' meat, I see."

"Yes," Dikkon said, "we have meat every Saturday."

There was a grunt and then a soft chuckle at this, though Dikkon failed to see what was amusing in such a plain statement of fact.

"I wanted to ask you . . . ," he began again.

But when he looked up, he had only a fleeting glimpse of the stranger darting through the open doorway.

Dikkon, amazed, glanced at the clock which hung on the wall. It was only half past eight. Never before had the other departed so early. Never before had he left without some sort of farewell.

And Dikkon leaped over the counter and stood in the doorway.

Already the stranger had disappeared in the trees of the square. He must have gone in that direction, for he had not had time to turn a corner, and the street was empty, up and down.

Dikkon peered earnestly across the square. What had been an old Spanish mission was now, with many additions, a huge grain and hay warehouse. It filled all the far side of the square, and the face of it, as always at night, was blank and black, with hardly a window to twinkle against the stars. There was nothing else to see, except the narrow valley at the right, which opened on the front of the Jordan Lodging House, three stories high—the biggest and the best in the town.

One window in it was lighted.

Dikkon went back and sat down in the chair where the stranger had lately been. From that viewpoint, the landscape was still more narrowed, and all that he could see was the shoulder of the warehouse, and the lighted window of the lodging house.

For some moments he remained in deep thought. It occurred to the awakened mind of Dikkon that the manner of the stranger always had been most unusual. Always that chair was placed in the same position. Always Prentiss stared constantly out into the night, as intently as a man reading a book. He would hardly take away his attention long enough to throw a side glance at Dikkon.

The light in the boarding-house window now went out, and Dikkon returned to his work, and thence he climbed to his bed. He had an odd feeling that he never would see Sam Prentiss again.

He was up, as usual, in the gray of the first light, cooked the breakfast porridge, ate his share, and went down hastily to the workroom, for Sunday never was an idle day. Uncle Charles, as usual, took a brief walk to begin the day. It was longer than usual on this occasion, and when he came back, he had an unusual gleam in his eyes.

"Trouble's starting loose in this town of ours

again," he declared. "They killed a man last night."

Dikkon waited. He had learned that questions rarely elicited extra information from Uncle Charles.

"Over in the Jordan place," Bender went on at last. "You can see the broken window right from our door."

IV

There was one difference between Sunday and the other days: no evening work. So, in the evening, Dikkon went out into the street and drifted by instinct, as it were, straight toward the Jordan Lodging House. It was dusk and after supper, so there was a considerable group of men gathered on the corner, while small hosts of children played on the verge of the street, or gathered to gape and stare and listen to the words of their elders.

Dikkon drifted uncertainly here and there. No one paid any attention to him. No one ever did. In this manner he picked up bits of news, and afterward he sauntered down the street, putting the odds and ends into one related tale.

Dan Hodge was the dead man. A gun had exploded in the room of Isidore Bernstein, on the third floor of the building, and by sheerest chance the deputy sheriff, Steve Martin, at that moment was climbing the stairs to join a party on the floor beneath. He heard the boom of the gun, went to inquire, and arrived in time to see men tumbling out the window. When he lighted a match, he found Dan Hodge dead on the floor.

What was the motive?

There might be dozens of motives. Dan Hodge was a bad man. He was so very bad that no one felt compunction on hearing of his departure from this world. No one sighed. No head was shaken.

Dan had lived by crooked cards and crooked guns. He had lived hard and he had lived fast. He had robbed, cheated, tricked, swindled, murdered, and, as a result of his crimes, had never spent a day in jail, never been fined a penny, and finally had settled down as a cowpuncher near the town.

His reputation was so exceedingly black that no one dared to touch him. He was said to work fairly well. Men liked to employ him, because it was felt that rustlers would not dare to poach where Dan Hodge might ride out on their trail.

Anyone who had been robbed, tricked, cheated, plundered by Dan might have come back for revenge. Anyone who had a friend that had fallen under the guns of Dan might have done this shooting. There was only one person who was not suspected, and that was Isidore Bernstein.

It appeared that he was a little, smooth-faced,

fat-bodied man, yellow of skin, smoky of eyes. Since the moment of the shooting he never had stopped shaking. He insisted on being taken to the jail, because he felt safe only when there were bars between him and the world.

It was not so much the details about Dan Hodge that Dikkon was interested in as one expression which he heard over and over again.

"They all get it."

"They" meaning the ruffians, the gunfighters.

Instances were given. There was Kid Noonan. He'd lived until he was fifty-five. But he "got it." A knife in the back had finished him.

There was St. Louis Joe Smith. He'd gone down after twenty years of retirement from guns and gunmen.

Hank Wilder swore off all evil courses and became a preacher. Hank Wilder was shot as he mounted into the pulpit one day.

"You live by guns, you die by guns."

Someone in the crowd had said that, and it rang in the ears of Dikkon. Sam Prentiss, he shrewdly suspected, lived by guns. Dikkon always thought of three things at once, when he considered Sam. That is to say, he saw the keen eyes, the long, lean hands, and the butts of the guns by which they dangled. One twitch of the fingertips and those guns would be conjured out of their holsters.

Sam Prentiss had much to do with guns. Certainly, Sam Prentiss had something to do with

164

the death of Dan Hodge. There was a spider-thread of suspicion which might lead, when investigated, to a strong cable of proof. Dikkon was not interested in following the clue. He was not at all interested. Merely to think of doing so made chills curdle in the small of his spine.

He went back to the shop and climbed to his room. There he sat on the edge of his bed, when he had undressed, and considered himself. He was not a very athletic figure. His stomach was soft in spite of hard fare. His knee bones stuck out. The calves of his legs hung flabby and cold. But his hands were different. They were, as Prentiss had pointed out, things of steel, and, as he also had suggested, they might be good with guns.

Dikkon shook his head violently and huddled into a nightgown, blew out the lamp, and rolled into the blanket. Sheets were considered a foolish luxury in the house of Uncle Charles.

He lay awake for a while with thoughts running rapidly through his mind, never stopping to be inspected. But there was a distinct connection between those who live by the gun and his own hands. It worried him. He decided that he would not get that revolver, after all, for what fool will tempt his fate?

When he went to sleep, he dreamed that Sam Prentiss came in and sat down in the usual chair. But he did not look through the open door. He fixed a side glance on Dikkon and said: "Do you think I had anything to do with the murder?"

Dikkon could not answer, in his dream.

Sam Prentiss stood up and leaned his hands on the counter.

"You suspect something," he said, and his eyes went into Dikkon's heart like two gimlets.

"I don't suspect anything," Dikkon said in his vision.

At that, Sam Prentiss smiled in such cold, cruel disbelief that Dikkon burst into a violent cold sweat.

It wakened him. He found the gray morning in the room and he was still cold and trembling in his bed.

It seemed that the sun would never come out, bright and strong, that morning. But at last breakfast was ended, and Dikkon sat again on his workbench. He was vastly glad to be there. Everything that was familiar was gladdening to the eye—even the worn leather seats on the bench, rubbed in streaks from black to shining brown. The smell of the leather, the innumerable small scraps from cuttings, the well-worn tools pleased him. They made him feel secure. Outside, the world was cold and dangerous, but behind the dusty windows of the shop there was peace and security.

Suddenly Uncle Charles said: "How much money you gotta have?"

He said it sullenly, and Dikkon was about to say: "I don't want any money, and I wouldn't have any money." But he checked himself. He was ashamed to admit that he was afraid to have money in his pocket. Uncle Charles would have thought him mad.

So he said: "I want fifty dollars."

"Fifty dollars!" wailed Bender.

Dikkon was silent. He hardly knew why he had named such a sum.

"There you go sulkin'!" Uncle Charles exclaimed. "Gloomin' and sulkin'! It ain't no longer possible to live with you no more. You make life miserable to me."

And he got down off the bench and went away.

He came back in an hour and counted ten five dollar bills into the hands of Dikkon. It seemed a fortune!

Then he pressed a bony forefinger into the breast of the boy.

"They're gonna sell Hodge's things at the auction room," he said secretly. "You go down there. Pick up a Colt mighty cheap, Dikkon. You go down there right now. Don't you wait. They'll be making the sale, pretty soon. Go along!"

Dikkon did not want to go, but he was pushed out of the shop.

"I can show you how to save money," Uncle Charles said, rubbing his hands together in glee.

The wind darted cold and sudden down the

street, and Dikkon gritted his teeth to harden his spirit. Then he went hastily forward because he would have been ashamed to turn around and say: "I don't want anything to do with guns. I want to live safe and warm in the shop."

He went slowly, slowly down the street until he came to the auction room. It was a sad place, where ragged, battered furniture was often offered for sale, and there was a yard behind, filled with rusting junk. Now he found a dense crowd there.

There was offered for sale a bony mustang, which stood in the street. There was also offered a saddle, as worn as the horse. A bridle. A good pair of spurs. A slicker and set of blankets. A Winchester of old make. Two Colts.

That completed the list. The sale already had opened. The auctioneer was trying to work up a little enthusiasm. He was a useless old man who spent every penny he made on liquor. He had had a wife and family, but they had cast him out, he was so utterly worthless. But he knew how to talk at an auction, and now he was making a little speech and trying to induce the crowd to become interested.

He said that this was one of the greatest opportunities which, so far as he knew, ever had come in the way of a man in that town. They had a chance to buy the relics of a man who would go down as a famous warrior of the frontier. He himself wished that he could buy any one of the items. He wished that he were not so old. He only wished that he could sit in Dan Hodge's saddle on the back of Hodge's horse with the weapons of Hodge in his hands.

"I'll lend you a quarter, Bill," said a wag. "Then you can have the whole outfit."

People laughed at this silly remark, but Dikkon did not laugh. He thought that there was something dreadful and disrespectful in thus disposing of the effects of the dead man. Particularly his guns. He had lived by those guns. They had kept him for so many years. They were almost more of the dead man than his flesh and blood had been.

Then the horse itself was auctioned off. It sold for fifteen dollars.

"The poor old spavined cripple," was the comment. "What you gonna do with it, Jud? They ain't three dollars' worth of dog feed in him."

The saddle went next. The rifle and bridle were disposed of. A revolver went for five dollars even. There were two. Dikkon thought he would wait until the first one had gone before he began bidding. The second was offered.

"I'll bid four bucks," said a rather familiar voice.

He looked hastily across the crowd. It was Sam Prentiss, who had stepped out from a corner of the wall.

V

It sent a shock through Dikkon.

Partly because he was seeing the man in daylight. Then, again, it seemed a terrible thing that Prentiss—if he had had a hand in the killing—should be here to buy a relic of the dead. It was like collecting a scalp that he had not had time to pause and snatch the night of the killing.

"Sam Prentiss offers me four dollars," said the auctioneer. "Now, there's a man that had ought to know a gun when he sees it. Four dollars is offered for this gun, and by a man that wants it bad, and his name is Sam Prentiss. Does anybody offer me five?"

"I will," Dikkon said.

He looked not at the auctioneer, but at Prentiss, and the quick eyes of the latter flashed at him through the crowd. They were like two glinting bits of metal.

That was only a quick glance, however.

"Good!" the auctioneer exclaimed. "Dog-gone me if it ain't Bender's boy! He's gonna shoot his way through the shoe leather, after this. Five dollars he says. And now, Prentiss, what you gonna do?"

"I'll make it a half," Prentiss said, and yawned.

"Six," Dikkon said promptly.

For he had felt, instantly, that the yawn of Prentiss was forced.

The auctioneer expanded like a flower in the sun.

"Dog-gone me if I noticed it before," he said. "Here's a gun that's got five niches filed into its handle. Five. Five dead men, my children. Who's gonna let that gun go so cheap? Why, this here is a gun that can't miss! That's why Prentiss wants it. Are you gonna let a real relic like this go so cheap?"

"Seven dollars!" a third man called out.

"And a half," said Prentiss.

"Why," someone remarked, "the old gun is full of wabbles, ain't it?"

"Eight," Dikkon said, a little shrill of voice.

"Well, I knew Hodge," Prentiss was heard to say. "I don't mind paying ten bucks for the thing merely as a keepsake."

"Ten!" shouted the auctioneer. "Ten's offered. You, young fellow?" He pointed at Dikkon.

"Eleven," Dikkon said.

People were beginning to look at him. He grew a little red, but he was determined. Prentiss wanted it. Prentiss knew guns. And at eleven dollars it was a great deal cheaper than a new weapon.

"Fifteen!" Prentiss barked, as though angered. And he turned and glared at Dikkon.

Dikkon dared not meet that glance. He felt his eyes staring.

"Sixteen!" he said rather hoarsely.

There was a laughing cheer.

"Let him have it," Prentiss declared.

And he turned and walked through the crowd, shouldering his way. Dikkon found himself counting out money.

"Use it better than Hodge did," the auctioneer was advising him. "Use it on quail."

The by-standers laughed again, but Dikkon walked away with the Colt, half frightened and half delighted. He had the gun in his coat pocket. It was far too big to be contained there, so he kept his hand on the butt of it, working his fingers on the handle. It seemed to Dikkon to fit marvelously well, and the roughness of the handle was reassuring to his fingertips.

"That gun's loaded, kid," said a quiet voice beside him.

Sam Prentiss was walking at his shoulder.

"Hello!" Dikkon exclaimed, startled.

"Lemme see if it ain't loaded," said Prentiss, holding out his hand.

Dikkon looked not at the extended hand but at the lean face of Prentiss, and it seemed to him that the other was a little white, and that his nostrils expanded and quivered as though in excitement. Yet Prentiss was trying to control himself. He was trying with such violence that he even forced a smile to his lips. He wanted that gun.

He wanted it so badly that Dikkon could not help wondering why he had let the weapon go so cheaply. However, the thing was done. No doubt he wanted it, and he wanted it for some great and good reason. There were differences between guns. Dikkon could not have lived so long in a Western town without learning much about firearms. There were differences, and, of course, men had their favorites.

Sam Prentiss knew about guns. With mysterious greed he wanted this one.

"It's just a Colt," Dikkon said.

"Don't I know that?" snapped Prentiss.

"Oh, sure you do."

"Lemme see it, will you?"

"Why?" Dikkon asked, clumsily fighting for time.

"Aw, I see." Prentiss nodded. "You think I'd do something to it? Steal it, maybe?"

He laughed, and the laughter rang so true that Dikkon hesitated.

"I knew Hodge," said Prentiss. "I knew him pretty well. We even rode on the same trails a couple of times. He wasn't such a bad gent. I want a keepsake of him."

"Why not the other gun?" Dikkon suggested. "That other fellow . . . he'd sell it pretty cheap, I think."

"Him? No, he wouldn't. Not the minute that he saw I really wanted it."

"Then why didn't you bid up this one?" asked Dikkon.

"I didn't want to make people think I was a fool. It ain't worth sixteen dollars. If I'd bid twenty, they would've laughed at me, and kept on laughing. But I don't mind telling you that I'll give you a neat little profit on that Colt. I'll pay you down twenty-five. And here you are."

He took a wallet from his pocket and sifted out five five-dollar bills.

"Thanks," Dikkon said, but making no effort to take the money. "I sort of like this gun, though."

"Why, you young fool," Prentiss exclaimed, heat appearing even in his voice, "it's an old, loose, wabbly thing. Hodge . . ."

Dikkon was greatly frightened. He was far from wanting to make this formidable fellow his enemy. But, at the same time, he did not wish to give up what seemed to be a prize, at least in the eyes of Prentiss.

"If it's no good, why did Hodge keep it?" he asked.

"Used to it. Felt it was luck," said Prentiss.

"And so do I," persisted Dikkon.

"You do? Look here. If you think I'm being foolish with you, try to hit something with it. Right yonder in the vacant lot there . . . see that new oil can. You got a loaded gun in your hand. Now see how straight it shoots."

174

"I will," Dikkon said fervently.

He knew very little about weapons. Certainly he was almost entirely unpracticed. But of what value was the gun to him, unless it actually had some extraordinary virtue. The earnestness of Prentiss at last impressed him. After all, it was quite probable that a man might wish to have a souvenir of a friend, an old companion.

He jerked the weapon suddenly from his pocket and fired almost blindly, the instant that it was clear.

To his own vast amazement, the oil can gave back a sharp and unmusical sound, and it tipped and fell slowly back with a clatter.

"Holy smoke!" Prentiss gasped.

He ran forward and raised the oil can. Even Dikkon could see in the distance that the face of the can was punctured fairly in the middle.

It thrilled him with joy and with wonder. This was to him a miracle. Even with a rifle he could not have been sure of striking even that broad mark, and that he should have nailed it with a mere revolver, and a snap shot at that, bewildered him.

It was plain that Prentiss was greatly impressed also. He came up with wonder in his eye.

"You've been foolin' with me, kid, I see," he said gravely. "You fire from the hip, eh?"

Dikkon made no reply.

"All right," Prentiss said, "if that old gat really

will shoot straight, I'll raise the ante a little. I'd even pay you forty dollars for the gun, kid."

Dikkon smiled.

Suppose someone had offered King Arthur its weight in gold for Excalibur, would not the hero have smiled? So Dikkon smiled now. It was no mere Colt that he held in his hand. It was a magic weapon.

He would not have said that he actually believed in magic. It was simply that he felt in the gun a mysterious quality. At least, no skill of his had struck the can!

"I wouldn't sell it," he said. "But, look here. I wish that you'd let me know why you didn't bid higher for the gun back there at the auction."

Anger at last mastered the remnant of diplomacy in Sam Prentiss. He snapped his fingers in Dikkon's face.

"Shut up, you, with your questions," he said. "You spy! You sneak! You . . . I'll see you to the devil before I'm through with you."

Dikkon put his back to the wall as though a dog had sprung at him, and then he watched Prentiss, who was already walking down the street with a long and restless stride. He could not accuse Prentiss of being a fool. But if he were not a fool, then he was something perilously close to a madman!

Dikkon did not wait there in the street.

He went home with a wildly beating heart

and the haste of one who carries with him an enormous treasure. He hurried to the shop and through it without a word to Uncle Charles. In his own room he settled down and laid the gun on the table before him.

VI

It was no mere mechanism of steel and wood. For Dikkon leaned above it until he distinguished the row of five notches, filed deeply into the handle of the weapon. That meant five lives taken with that gun, and such a small engine of destruction must, it seemed, be endowed with a peculiar malice, a peculiar faculty before it could achieve such results.

Now, while he went on with his examination, he found the room dimmed, as though the bright sky had been sheeted across with clouds, and turning curiously from the table, he saw in the window a powerful man with low, beetling brow, and a face like a great, square fist.

He was the most formidable man that Dikkon ever had seen. A bulldog would have winced away from that ugly face, the upper lip furled back from the pointed teeth. He had a revolver pointed at Dikkon and now he said with savage emphasis: "Hand over that gun, kid! Be quick or I'll blow your block off."

Dikkon blinked at a spinning world. He hardly heard the words of the stranger, certainly he did not attach any meaning to them. All that he was aware of was the black mouth of the gun which looked at him, and in a dreadful panic, he thought that his last moment had come.

He did what a frightened lap dog will sometimes do when a great mastiff growls at it. Extremity of terror made Dikkon run at the stranger.

The gun boomed heavily. The noise flooded through the room so that Dikkon was sure the ball had torn through his vitals. Then he reached the window and flung his lean, hard fists into the face of the man.

Blindly, with all his force, once, twice, and again he struck. And the gun boomed regularly in response. What Dikkon in his blind panic did not see was that the intruder had become wedged tightly in the window. The gun he had drawn was jammed against the wood of the frame so that it could not be moved a hair's breadth.

The more he struggled, the tighter he was fixed in place, for it was a narrow little window that looked in upon Dikkon's attic room.

"Hey, you . . . help! Hold on!" shouted the stranger. "You . . . help! I give up!"

Dikkon's first two punches had gone home with weight. The third clipped luckily that spot which is called "the button."

The stranger relaxed, and relaxing fell backward from the window, letting his gun drop with a rattle on the floor of the room. He rolled over and over down the roof, until his foot lodged in the gutter and stopped his fall. Then, with a yell, like a great cat he clambered lightning-fast along the gutter and swung down over the side of the building.

The mist of terror cleared from the eyes of Dikkon. He could look down as far as the street, and there he saw a crowd hastily assembling and pointing up toward him. A horseman went by, streaking dust behind. There was a shout. A gun barked twice. And presently Dikkon saw the sheriff returning on his horse up the street, herding before him a man whose hands were held above his head.

Crimson streaked the face of this man. It looked as though he had been shot through the head.

Then it seemed to Dikkon that the captive was singularly like the man who had blocked the window, just the moment before.

Thunder sounded on the stairs. Dikkon picked up the fallen gun of the stranger. Two chambers were loaded. Hodge's gun he dropped into his coat pocket, and noticed as he did so that his hands were covered with blood, just as the door of his room was cast open and half a dozen men crowded in the doorway.

They spilled awkwardly back at the sight of the gun in Dikkon's hand.

"Are you nicked?" asked one, who clung to his place, with a very frightened face.

"Of course not," Dikkon said.

"He ain't hurt!" exclaimed the stranger.

"He ain't hurt!" said a voice farther down the stairs. "Jerry Bulger comes and empties a gun at him, and he ain't hurt!"

"Dikkon! Dikkon!" yelled the voice of Uncle Charles.

"Coming!" Dikkon said.

He went down the stairs, rather embarrassed by the red stains on his hands. Those who had rushed up to him pressed back against the walls on either side to let him pass. There seemed to be respect, even awe, in their faces.

At the foot of the stairs, his uncle seized on him with trembling hands.

"You gone and got yourself killed! Look at your hands! Look at your hands! What good are you to me with your hands all smashed up?"

"My hands are all right," Dikkon said. "I'll wash them."

He had no time to wash them, however. For just then the deputy sheriff, Steve Martin, appeared in the door of the shop, ushering before him the man of the battered face.

It was, beyond doubt, he who had appeared in the window. He was breathing hard, and bore a cut beneath his left eye and a smashed nose.

"Hey, you . . . young Dikkon!" Steve Martin said. "What's been happening here?"

"I dunno," said Dikkon.

Those who had gone up to his room to investigate now swarmed back and crowded the shop. Others thronged behind Martin and blocked the door. The town was turning out.

Many voices began to talk at once, telling the deputy, but the latter shouted them down.

"I'll get enough of you for witnesses. You, Dikkon, tell me what happened."

"Certainly," Dikkon said. "This man came to my window. I got him to go away again. That's all."

There was a murmur. Steve Martin frowned.

"What's the matter with you? Bulger, you gonna say anything? Or are you saving it for the judge?"

"Who's this bloke, I wanna know?" Bulger insisted. "I heard that he was a soft kid . . . a shoemaker."

"He is a shoemaker," Martin confirmed.

"That's a lie and the devil of a loud one," Bulger declared. "I'll tell you what . . . he's a pug!"

"Him?"

"Do I know a fighting man?"

"You been in the ring," the deputy sheriff said.

"He comes in at me," Bulger said, "with a straight left, on the jump. Then he flashes over a

181

right cross, and next he connects with a left shift that knocked me out of the window and near off the roof."

He rubbed his chin with the tips of his fingers.

"He's a pug!" persisted Bulger.

"Lemme hear from you, kid," Steve Martin said. "Why you tryin' to cover up this gent Bulger? Did he come into your window and turn loose a gun on you?"

"I suppose so," Dikkon answered.

"You suppose so!" sneered the deputy. "What do you suppose happened after that?"

"I seemed to strike him," Dikkon said.

"You seemed to? Didn't you have a gun?"

"Yes."

"Why didn't you use a gun on him?"

"I didn't want to hurt him, of course," Dikkon said more brightly.

"He didn't want to!" the lawman repeated to the crowd. "All he did was that!" And he pointed with a chuckle to the battered face of Bulger.

He added to Dikkon: "Supposings and thinkings ain't any good. You willing to swear to what happened in that room?"

Dikkon thought for a moment. As far as he could make out, that whole scene was now reduced to two points. The first was the appearance of Bulger in the window, with leveled gun. The second was the disappearance of Bulger. Exactly what else had happened, he hardly could tell. He thought that a gun had exploded many times. And there was blood on his hands.

"I couldn't swear to anything," Dikkon said frankly.

"Hey," called the deputy sheriff, "you young fool, ain't you gonna give me enough to let me jail this bird?"

"Jail him? Hasn't he had trouble enough?" Dikkon asked.

"Wait a minute!" barked Martin. "You know this bird? This is Jerry Bulger . . . this is *the* Jerry. I been waiting for five years to lay my hands on him. Now I got him, and you ain't gonna make a charge ag'in' him? Not even disturbing the peace?"

"I don't think so," Dikkon said slowly.

Jerry Bulger leaned against the wall and gasped. The crowd gasped as well.

While Steve Martin exclaimed: "It don't make no difference that this here gunman is on your trail?"

It did make a difference, of course, but Dikkon was not able to think around all of the corners of this problem. He wanted to be at peace and alone in the shop.

"Are you through with me?" Dikkon asked.

"Well, this here beats me," the deputy sheriff asked. "I got half an idea that you've been a snake in the grass all the time, kid. You've been throwing in with the thugs, have you? Is that it?

And now you won't split on your pal, Bulger? Is that it?"

Dikkon returned no answer. The townsmen seemed enthralled with interest.

"Is that all you got to say to Bulger?" the sheriff shouted.

"Oh, no," said Dikkon. "I guess he'd better have this back. It's your gun, I think," he said, and handed over the captured Colt to the gunman.

Bulger received it with amazement so great that he could not speak.

"Is that all?" cried the angered deputy.

He turned on his heel and stroke away.

"You can go free . . . and to Jericho with this town!" cried Steve Martin to no one in particular and to all within earshot. "You fools love the crooks. I'm gonna find me a new home!"

It seemed a very grim speech to Dikkon. The other townsmen filed out of the shop in silence. They stood about outside, murmuring. He was left inside with his uncle and Bulger, the gunman, whose returned weapon was now stowed away in his clothes.

VII

It seemed to Dikkon that he had closed himself in a trap. He looked to Jerry Bulger with alarm, but the latter, after staring for a moment, turned on his heel and followed the sheriff.

Dikkon took his seat on the workbench.

He and his uncle went on until noon, with never a word. Perhaps an hour later, right before he went off to lunch, Charles Bender muttered: "Trouble has broke loose."

The days of the week drifted by, but they went with thrice the celerity with which they had moved of old. There was hardly an hour a day when strangers or townsmen were not coming into the shop. All the strangers wanted to be introduced to Dikkon. They shook hands with him with enthusiasm. They chatted until his continued silence stopped them.

And, among other things, they left many orders.

Uncle Charles, who had looked upon all this disturbance and notoriety as a calamity at the first, instantly clapped on a twenty-five percent increase in his prices. And he noticed with amazement that the flood of new orders was undiminished.

He passed into a hysteria of joy. Smiles uprooted

his usual settled darkness of countenance. He was even heard to chuckle now and again.

And on Friday he said to Dikkon: "I gotta get a couple of good men in here. I gotta hire that next shop and knock a hole through the wall. Boy, the time has come when we gotta expand. We can't handle the orders that we got."

This was astonishing news. Expansion had always been the old man's dread.

However, Saturday came, and found Dikkon more restless than ever he had been before. It made little difference that new faces constantly were drifting into the shop and out again. The point was that he had not satisfied the new taste for excitement that had been awakened in him. And beyond the dull panes of his window, he guessed continually at a delightful world that had not been revealed.

Over the course of the day there had been twenty visitors, at least. There had been eight new orders on that day alone. In the evening the usual quiet began, but Dikkon, listening with extraordinary sharpness, could hear happy voices that tingled in the distance, voices in cheerful dispute, and laughter that turned corners and faded suddenly beyond his ken.

Eight o'clock came, and at that instant there was a footfall on the street that paused and turned in at his shop. The hair rose a little on Dikkon's head.

Was Sam Prentiss returning to wait for the death of another man?

It was not Sam Prentiss. It was a woman. As she came within the sphere of the lamp Dikkon saw that she was not even a woman. She was a young girl of eighteen or nineteen. She was so beautiful, fresh, and fair, that she brought back the morning of the day, as it were. She brushed the weariness from Dikkon.

She wanted a pair of boots made. Low boots, to wear under leggings. Could Dikkon make them?

He shook his head. He had made boots for women before this, but they were the wild-riding women of the range, tough as men, and very different from this girl.

She seemed very disappointed. There was no other place to which she could go. Everyone said that he was the best shoemaker in the town.

"You could try," she said with hope in her voice.

"I could try," admitted Dikkon.

She sat down in the corner chair and braced herself. But though the riding boot she wore seemed to fit to a delicate nicety, yet it came off at once, slipping easily. Dikkon was not surprised. The other boot followed. Now, placed side by side, they looked ridiculously small, like the boots of a child. He wondered at the wrinkles across the base of the toes. Something tickled Dikkon, and he began to fight back a chuckle.

She stood up in her stockinged feet on the paper that he had spread, and he made the outlines, drawing them in very carefully. The enthusiasm of an artist-shoemaker seized him. He told himself that he would make those the finest shoes that ever had walked out of the shop. He knew a calfskin in their stock, a little too thin for a man's boots, but supple as silk, and of strong quality. That should be for her.

Then he took the strip of measuring paper and checked it for the measurements around the toes, the instep, the heel, the ankle. He measured the calf of the leg, and stood up, blushing hotly.

She was perfectly indifferent. He hurried behind the counter lest she should see his redness of face and despise him for it. He felt that if he only could resume his place on the workbench, his composure would return.

She had drawn on her riding boots again with ridiculous ease—how men grunted and groaned over the same job—and now she lingered at the counter and looked at him.

Could he tell her the way to Logan Creek?

He closed his eyes and let the image of her clear away.

"You go right out on the Loringham Road," he began.

"Which road is that?" she asked.

"Don't you know the town?"

"I just came in today. I've got to go on tonight."

"Not tonight!"

"Yes. I have to."

"But Logan Creek's pretty wild, you know!"

"Is it?"

"Terrible," he affirmed. "You gotta sort of fumble for the trail even in the daylight."

"I'll have to get a guide," the girl said, and sighed.

"There's a pretty good hotel here," he told her.

"Oh, I couldn't stay."

She lowered her eyes in thought. She raised them again and they were filled with trouble.

"Is there any regular guide in the town?" she asked.

"Guide? I dunno of any," answered Dikkon.

She sighed.

"I'd better give you my name," she said. "For the boots, you know."

Dikkon poised his pencil above a piece of paper.

"Edith Murray."

"You ain't Mister John Murray's daughter?"

"I'm his niece."

He looked at her blankly. Only rich people could have a daughter like this girl—all velvet! Only rich people could afford her! Not that her clothes were very expensive, but it was the quality of the girl who wore them. Like a thoroughbred horse—dainty, delicate, and strong!

He wondered at her a moment, wondered,

indeed, how she could dream of such a wild ride as that up Logan's Creek—and at night! For Dikkon's own part, he happened to know the trail by mere chance, having gone that way on three different occasions during his infrequent trips into the country. He himself would not have dreamed of going by such a trail in the darkness. It made him rather cold to think of it. For that matter, he hated even the trip from his shop to his room, in the dark. Even when he was carrying the night lantern up. Something always seemed to be following behind, and waiting before.

"You're Mister Murray's niece," he echoed.

"You couldn't name a safe guide for me?"

"I don't know many people in the town very well," Dikkon said, worried.

"I don't know what to do," said the girl. "I . . . I suppose that I'll manage some way. . . ."

He tried to think of something to say, but his tongue was tied. He merely could follow her to the door, yearning over her slenderness, her light and graceful step.

"Are both those horses yours?" asked Dikkon.

For he saw two beautiful animals with starred foreheads outside in the night, two pairs of big, bright eyes.

"One belongs to Cousin Charlie. He came in with me today. But he had to take the train down the valley."

"To Charming?"

"Yes."

"But that's up the valley."

"Oh, yes," she said.

Then he suggested: "It's near eleven miles. You'd better go to the hotel."

"Poor Uncle John. He'd worry frightfully," she said.

She stepped onto the board sidewalk and tilted back her head, exclaiming: "It's such a beautiful night! See that planet!"

He followed her gaze. It seemed to Dikkon that a fragrance blew in the wind as he gazed at the wild beauty of the stars above them.

"That's not a planet," he told her.

She was so close to him as she turned that her shoulder touched his breast. She looked up into his face.

"Isn't it?" she asked.

He steadied himself a little.

"No, that's Arcturus."

"Arcturus! It's so big!"

"It's the biggest star in our sky."

"Is it?"

It was delicious to be able to give her facts.

"Yes. It's in Boötes. Arcturus in the heel of the hand. You see? The others are like the tips of fingers."

"You know a great deal," observed Edith Murray.

"I only know a little. But I pick things up . . . hear conversations," he said.

"Oh," she said.

"Then you sit on the bench all day and what you've read or seen . . . it soaks in. You think things over. I wonder about a guide," Dikkon said.

"You couldn't go?" she asked.

"I go? Leave the shop? Oh, good heavens, no!" cried Dikkon.

He had not expressed half the horror of the idea. The sensation was still traveling down through unplumbed depths of dread. What would Uncle Charles say to such a thing?

VIII

She stood between the heads of the horses. They towered high above her. They turned to her from either side and sniffed gently at her cheeks. They loved her, it seemed. Of course they loved her!

"I can manage, then," said the girl.

"I'll get you somebody," he said.

"I wouldn't want just anybody," she said. "You know . . . it's a long ride at night. I'd have to have someone I could trust."

"I . . . ," began Dikkon.

Then he paused, retasting that sentence of hers,

because it suggested delightfully that she trusted him. She would have been glad enough to have him go along with her.

"If you could just show me how the way begins," she urged.

"I'll show you."

He led her out to the middle of the street.

"You see that white glimmer? That's the church."

"The church," she repeated in a resolute tone, as of one who intended to remember.

"Then you turn to the left."

"The left," she echoed.

"Not the lane, but the road."

"The road."

"You go straight down the road about a quarter of a mile till you come to three partings of the way. You take the right-hand one. You keep along it till you come to a haystack on the right and a barn on the left. You take a bridle path that runs around the corner of the barn . . ."

"The barn," the girl said vaguely.

"Then you go along for about two miles, never turning away from the main trail."

"How shall I tell the main trail?"

"Because it's mostly pointing for Mount Cracker."

"Can I see Mount Cracker in the dark?"

"I don't suppose you can," admitted Dikkon, checked.

"Oh, dear," sighed the girl. Then she said bravely: "Well, I'll just try."

Then suddenly, she was in the saddle.

"Good night, Mister Dikkon," she said. "Thank you for your help."

"Wait!" shouted Dikkon.

He stood at the heads of the horses.

"Yes?" she said.

"You wait . . . I'll go with you," he cried.

"Oh, no."

"Oh, yes. I will."

"I couldn't let you come."

"I will come! I . . . just wait a little minute. I'll get my hat."

He darted in and caught it up. He made sure that the magic gun of Dan Hodge was in his pocket before he went to brave the terrors of the unknown darkness. Then he hurried out again.

There was nothing to be seen. She had flown!

No, just to the left . . . there she was!. His heart beat again. He sprinted after her.

"You mustn't go alone!" he begged her, once he caught up.

"I couldn't let you come," she insisted.

"Why not?"

"Your poor wife would miss you so."

"Wife?" Dikkon repeated, strangely staggered by the word. "Wife? But I have no wife."

"No?" she said in seeming surprise.

"Oh, no. I haven't a wife."

"Will you really come, then?"

"I will, I will," said Dikkon.

He caught the head of the other horse and in another moment he was riding down the street at her side. He was rather frightened by the gait of the horse. It went along with a step that seemed bounding even when it walked. And when it pranced, it seemed half flying.

Dikkon would have slipped to the ground at once, on any other occasion, but now there was something else that crowded into his brain and drove even fear into a most obscure corner.

"Mister Dikkon, you are so wonderfully kind."

"I'm not," Dikkon insisted. "I'm glad to come."

They had passed the church. They had turned down the road. The smell of the open fields rose sweetly to them.

Glad to go? She would not know. He would not try to explain to her that this was like riding through the fields of heaven!

"We must go back and tell your mother that you'll be late home," she said with a sudden cry of alarm.

"I have no mother," said Dikkon.

"Oh," Edith said.

Then she added: "Oh, poor boy. I'm so sorry!"

Tears of self-pity rushed into the eyes of Dikkon. But it was a divine pleasure to be pitied by such a girl.

They twisted past the corner of the barn. They

were launched now in the wilderness. Dark trees lifted enormous heads nearby, shutting out all but bright patches of the stars. When they looked back toward the town, they could see only the random yellow glimmer of a light here and there.

"You won't be very afraid?" Dikkon asked.

"Oh, no! Not with you. I heard about you."

"You heard about me?"

"Of course, everyone in town's talking about you. They told me that you're a tremendous hero, Mister Dikkon."

He tried to deny it, but his tongue stuck. His heart began to beat so fast that he was half stifled.

"They say that you don't care even if a man draws a gun on you. You go and knock him through windows and things."

"I don't, though. That was just an accident."

"Don't be so modest. I think it's wonderful," said the girl. "Shall we gallop?"

"If you want to."

Away she went. Dikkon took a desperate grip, but his horse, after tossing its head once or twice, began to bound away, lengthening its stride with sudden lurches. Dikkon was usually more out of the saddle than in it. Sometimes he seemed to be battering on bedrock. Sometimes he was afloat like a bird.

The girl drew up. He rushed past her and gradually managed to get the head of his mount. He was dizzy. His eyes were rolling. He was quite out of breath and bewildered when she came up beside him.

"Wasn't it lovely?" she said.

"Yes," gasped Dikkon.

They had covered two miles of trail. There loomed the entrance to Logan Cañon, fenced by two towers of granite a thousand feet high. All between was as black as pitch.

"You're not really afraid?" he asked her.

"Oh, no. Of course I'm not."

"You're wonderful!" Dikkon said. "It scares me a good deal."

"What on earth frightens you?"

"The cañon, you know."

"Does it? You're only joking, though."

"I'm not. I mean . . . it's dark and big. But don't you worry."

She made a little pause. He heard nothing but the crunching of the hoofs of the horses. What was she thinking?

"You see," broke out Dikkon, "everybody's mistaken about me. They think that I'm a hero. I'm not, though. I'm not a hero at all. Just some things happened. That was all."

"Ah, you're modest . . . I know," she answered wisely.

He did not attempt to argue the point any further.

They passed on up the cañon slowly. He had to take the lead, because the path turned and twisted here and there. Usually he did not remember a turning until he came straight upon it. Instinct helped him. Instinctive, buried memory rose up and showed him the way to go.

He had done very little riding in his life, and checking this spirited, high-blooded horse, riding continually into his stirrups, and leaning back against the reins, he began to grow sore. A pang began to drive into his left side, between the hip and the lowest rib. It passed gradually deeper. It was a sword, being thrust stroke by stroke through his body. It reached his spine. It went on. He was beginning to grow numb with torture.

"Is there much of this cañon?" asked the girl.

"Let's stop and rest a bit," Dikkon suggested.

"You're not tired, are you?"

"I am, a little."

"How strange!" she said.

He sighed. "I suppose it is," he admitted. "I'm not so very strong."

"You'd make yourself out nothing . . . not brave . . . not very strong . . . but you knock men through windows."

She clung to that fact, and he saw that it was useless to fight back against her strong conviction.

"There's another mile of the cañon," he told her.

She said no more.

They came out from the cañon to the high ground.

"Oh," she said suddenly, "I forgot about my flashlight. We could use that to fumble through the rocks, couldn't we?"

"It would just burn out," he said.

"Ah, but it's very strong."

Now it gleamed in her hand. Once, twice, and thrice strong flashes gleamed against the nearest trees. Dikkon's horse snorted and leaped aside.

By the time he had mastered it, she said: "We won't use it if you think we'd better not. It seems to frighten your horse."

"It does," Dikkon panted. "This h-h-horse . . . seems to h-have a d-d-devil in him."

She did not answer him at once.

He heard something muffled, but it was no more than a pulse of sound, like stifled sobbing— like stifled laughter, rather.

He decided that it could not be laughter— certainly it was not sobbing. For in a moment she began to sing aloud.

IX

The trail dipped from the hill into a continuation of the cañon, but it was the narrowest part of all, and so dark that the descent into it was like that down long stairs into a well. Dikkon had to ride and halt, ride and halt. He fairly crept down the descent, though as a matter of fact the way was not so very steep. It was only the enormous shafts of the pine trees, rising endlessly above them, and the grim shadows of the upper walls of the ravine that made that ride seem to be dipping down into the bowels of the earth. Dikkon kept his nerves steady with a hard effort. But once or twice he was on the verge of asking the girl to turn and go back with him to the town, since he could not be sure of the rest of the journey. But he had a chilly foreknowledge that if he suggested such a thing, she would laugh at him and ride on alone through the black night.

Never in his life had he felt less a hero. Never had the old battered shop and the worn leather seats on the workbench seemed so alluring. He came to a place where the trail narrowed almost to a point. The trees stood like vast brown walls, solid and ancient. Although the trail was narrow, it was smooth, and there seemed no reason why the girl should have fallen behind. But so she did, and as he came to a little runlet, with one star glittering on its dark face, he checked his horse and called to her to see if she were far away. She did not answer. Fear strangled Dikkon so that he could not call out a second time. But he swung his horse around and at the same time he heard a faint whistling sound. It was like the wind through trees, but sharper, cleaner cut, and nearer. He was distinctly aware of something dropping past his face, and then his arms were jerked against his sides by the noose of a rope. He heard it hiss like a snake as it was tightened. Then he was jerked from his saddle and landed with a great thud on his back.

The shock knocked every whit of breath from his body, but while his breath left him and his brain spun, he fumbled vaguely for the revolver. Even in that moment he had a mighty confidence that it would be able to extricate him from his peril.

He heard a loud voice shouting: "I got him clean. Come on, boys, and gimme a light to wind him up by!"

They brought a light. It was a small lantern that showed Dikkon to them, but it also showed their faces to Dikkon, and the first features he recognized were those of Prentiss. The second belonged to Jerry Bulger. The third man was a stranger, but he looked fully as grim as the other two.

Prentiss flashed the lantern in the face of Dikkon and laughed.

"The longest way round is the shortest way home. Is that right, kid?" he demanded. And at the same instant he leaned and drew the revolver from the holster at the side of Dikkon.

"Hold on!" exclaimed Bulger. "How do you get that way?"

The third man was busy tying the hands of Dikkon, who he now helped, still gasping for breath, to his feet.

"What do we do with this sap?" he asked. "Keep your eye on that gun, Jerry!"

"I ain't gonna eat it," declared Prentiss.

"You could lose it, though," answered the stranger sharply.

"Do you think that I'd double-cross you, Willie?" Prentiss complained sadly.

"In a minute, old son," replied Willie. "In a minute, if you thought that you could get away with it. What we gonna do with this sap?"

"Take him on to the clearing. Keep a gun jabbed into his back, will you?"

In that manner, Dikkon was brought through the trees. The muzzle of a Colt pressed uncomfortably against his spine. He was curtly assured that if he so much as stumbled, his backbone would be blown in two.

They went only a short distance, weaving among the trees, with the lantern throwing its light only part way up the vast brown trunks of the pines. The foliage began far above, like a low sky held up on pillars. Then they came into a little clearing. Across it ran the same little runlet by which Dikkon had paused only a moment before.

This had been the base of the attack. Three horses were tethered to the trees, their eyes glistening as they pricked their ears at the light. One of them even whinnied a low greeting, and the heart of Dikkon was eased a little. Men who could be kind to dumb beasts could not be too terrible to their brother men. Moreover, he was thankful that the girl was not with him at the moment of the capture. Edith Murray in the hands of these brutal fellows—that was unthinkable!

By this time she must have heard the noise. She would cower somewhere in the woods, sick with fear. But if she only waited for the light of day to come, she could extricate herself from the woods with no danger.

Someone suggested a fire, because it was growing cold and they had to talk things over. The flames rose at once. A few handfuls of pine needles started it. Twigs and brush were tossed on. Presently the clearing was awash with red waves that showed even the tops of the trees and made the distant stars seem dim.

Dikkon, looking up, saw Arcturus, and he smiled bitterly.

Willie made him sit down against a small stump. To that stump he lashed Dikkon securely.

"Have we got it, really?" he asked.

Prentiss and Bulger stood close together examining the revolver.

"We got it," they said.

At that, Willie ran in and joined them. All their

heads were bowed close together. There was silence. Then a gasp.

"We got it!" said the two of them together.

Presently they separated and fell back a little from one another, gasping as though they could hardly believe the good fortune that had come to them.

"You've had the care of that long enough, Prentiss," said Willie. "I'll guard it for a while."

"I don't believe you will, Tucker," Bulger contradicted. "It's my turn!"

"We'll put it on the ground by the fire, here," Prentiss said, making peace when it seemed that the other two would leap at the throats of one another.

He laid the gun on the ground. They made a circle around it. And Dikkon watched with understanding and appreciation. No doubt these were all hardened breakers of the law. To them the possession of such a gun was much to be desired. There was magic in it. The five notches were one proof. The desperate eagerness of the trio to possess it was another.

Suddenly Prentiss turned on Dikkon. "Kid, where'd you get the tip about this?"

"About what?" Dikkon asked.

"About that?" replied Prentiss, and pointed to the ground where the revolver lay.

Dikkon shrugged his shoulders. "I could see the five notches on it," he said.

"You wanted it because it had five notches on it?" Prentiss asked sharply.

"Well," Dikkon said, "why else do the rest of you want it?"

"He's got enough brass," said Willie Tucker.

"Maybe he means it," responded Prentiss.

"And maybe he don't," put in Bulger. "He ain't a fool. I'm telling you that!"

"Will you tell me how you knew that I was riding this way tonight?" Dikkon asked.

"Hey, ain't you tumbled yet?" Bulger asked.

"To what?"

"He don't savvy it yet," Bulger said, and laughed aloud.

The others laughed in turn, but more moderately. Dikkon did not seem to occupy much of their attention, but their greedy eyes turned back upon the ground and the gun which lay there, glimmering in the firelight.

"What're we gonna do with him?" asked Bulger.

"We'll settle that . . . after we've settled about this. Who carries the gun?"

"I will," Prentiss said. "I guess you can trust me."

"Listen, Sam, don't be a fool," advised Willie Tucker.

"Would you be safer with it than me?" Prentiss asked, narrowing his eyes.

"Maybe not. Lemme hear from you, Jerry."

"I'll take the gun," said Bulger. "Never double-crossed partners in my life."

Prentiss laughed softly, and Bulger winced and said no more.

"Well, we ain't gonna leave it here. I hope," said Willie Tucker.

"Sit down and we'll think it over."

They sat down on their heels, and the red fire stained their faces. They pushed back their hats. Their tousled hair fell down over their foreheads. They looked to Dikkon the most formidable trio he ever had seen.

And he felt that they were tensed and ready to spring at one another, like three dogs crouched around a bone, every one of them willing to die for the sake of it, but each hesitant to begin such a deadly affray. With terror and with awe, Dikkon watched them, wondering what would become of him afterward? He was terribly afraid. But at least he could thank fate that he had not led the girl into the hands of these scoundrels.

Even as he thought of her, she materialized out of the shadows among the trees. He could not believe it. It did not seem possible that she would dare to walk out on that formidable circle. But then, poor child, having lost her way, would she not go fearlessly toward the first light, never dreaming that there was evil in human nature?

Slender and small, she paused a moment by the trees and then walked forward, leading her horse.

"Go back!" Dikkon shouted. "Go back! Mount your horse! Ride, ride! These men are devils!"

She did not even hesitate. She walked straight on toward the fire.

X

Suddenly Willie Tucker began to laugh loudly.

"He's warning away the girl," he cried.

Straight past Dikkon Edith Murray went and halted to make a fourth member of the group.

"You got it all right?" she asked.

How sweet and soft was her voice.

"There it lies," said Willie Tucker.

"How does it look?"

"See for yourself," replied Tucker.

"I don't know so well about such things. You tell me, Sam. You're an expert."

"It looks fifty or sixty thousand to me."

The girl whistled. "That'll do," she said.

"For pin money," chuckled Prentiss.

Dikkon stared and stared. He would not believe it. He could not believe that she was a part and portion of this gang. But, with a sinking heart, he remembered how she had insisted upon his guidance, and how, at the head of the last ravine, she had flashed the torch three times. His heart seemed to turn to lead.

She abandoned her horse and came to him. Unabashed, cheerful, she stood before him.

"I'm sorry, Lew," she said. "But business is business, eh?"

That was her only expression of regret, if it could be called an apology, and Dikkon looked after her as she retreated, trying to make himself understand, with a stunned mind which refused to act.

She stood beside the fire now, as fresh, as dainty, as childish as when she had come into his shop that evening.

"The girl'll carry the gun," Prentiss suggested eagerly.

"All right." Edith nodded and leaned to pick up the Colt.

"Hold on!" yelled Jerry Bulger.

She straightened and stepped back.

"I can hear fairly well, Jerry," she said. "You don't have to shout."

"What do you want?" snarled Prentiss. "Ain't Eddie square enough? Ain't she a lady?"

"Aw, she's all right," Jerry said. "I ain't ag'in' you, Eddie," he apologized to her. "I like you fine. Only . . . I never seen a fifty-thousand-dollar lady in my life before, and I don't expect to see one now. Let that gun lie, I say!"

"It won't walk home on its own legs," the girl

said, smiling, perfectly composed in the face of this protest. "You boys settle it any way you want." She turned away. She began to hum.

"Drop the gun for a minute," went on Prentiss. "Let's decide on Dikkon."

The girl turned back.

"Tap him on the head and leave him lie," Bulger suggested. "He's too dangerous to leave alive, after we clear out."

"He is," agreed Prentiss.

"Dangerous? I dunno that he looks dangerous," said Willie Tucker. "He come out of the saddle quick enough."

"Dangerous? Don't be silly," said the girl. "The poor boy's a lamb!"

Dikkon blushed.

"Lamb, is he?" Jerry Bulger sneered. "Look at my face?"

"You stick yourself in a window and let him punch your face off," replied the girl. "Does that show he's dangerous?"

"Tie up that kind of talk, Eddie," Prentiss advised. "Don't get Jerry mad for nothing. I say that the kid is a bad one. He's a young bird, but a tough one. I seen him shoot a gun from the hip and make a bull's-eye at fifty yards. Nothin' slicker I ever seen, and I've watched all the big ones at work."

"Did he do that?" asked the girl. She wandered slowly toward Dikkon.

"You'd promise to keep off the trail?" she asked. "If we let you go free . . . would you promise to keep off our trail?"

"Let him go free?" yelled Willie Tucker. "I don't say that. But leave him tied to the stump yonder."

"That's only another way of killing him," answered the girl.

"Look here," barked Prentiss. "Have you fallen for the shoemaker, Eddie?"

"More for the shoemaker than for the yegg," she retorted coldly.

"You've come here to talk poison, have you?" Prentiss demanded, striding over and looking darkly down upon her.

"Listen, Sammie," Edith said, "you can't bluff me. I know you. You don't frighten me at all with that sort of stuff. And furthermore," she added, "if you start another line of talk like this, I'll let Chuck know about it. That's that."

She walked past Prentiss and stood closer to the fire. It seemed to Dikkon that the rosy light poured through her. Hers was a rich and translucent beauty.

"Let's talk sense," she said now. "This poor boy, Dikkon . . . I never ran into any one so simple. I was ashamed to take him along. Believe me, I was."

Dikkon grew a hotter red than he was before.

"That's pretty talk, and that's sweet talk," said Bulger, "but it's fool talk. That kid's dangerous. He's gotta go down."

"We gotta finish him," Prentiss declared with equal force.

Willie Tucker's was the only friendly voice besides the girl's, and Dikkon waited feverishly to hear his judgment. It was mere indifference.

"You boys have seen more of the gent than I have," Tucker said. "Suppose we draw straws to have him bumped off?"

"We'll do that," Bulger and Prentiss agreed enthusiastically. "The long straw loses. The long straw does the killing. Fix some straws for us, Eddie. We gotta get out of this."

"Do you mean that you'd murder him?" she asked, incredulous.

"Aw, look here," Prentiss responded, "don't put it that way. We're just using a streak of sense. That's all."

"I'll never let you do it!" she cried, stamping her foot.

Dikkon drew a great breath and sat up straight against his bonds.

"You won't let us do it?" Prentiss drawled with contempt.

"Sam," she cried in feverish earnest, "listen to me. I tell you what. I can raise money enough to make it worth your while."

"That's fairly good," Willie Tucker said. "I

don't see much danger in this here frightened shoemaker."

"You don't know him," answered Prentiss. "You never saw him before."

"That's true." Tucker nodded. "Well, have it your own way. I don't give a care. You fix the straws, Prentiss."

"I'll fix them well enough."

"I'll . . . I'll turn you in for murder!" gasped Edith.

"Listen, Eddie. Don't be a fool," Prentiss said. "We ain't askin' you to take your chance at drawin' the straws, are we?"

"Are you dead set?" she asked.

"Of course we are."

"It's the most wicked thing I ever heard of. I brought him into this murder trap! Sam, I tell you on my word of honor, he's just a simple country boy. He's hardly more than a half-wit!"

And, as she spoke, she whirled away from them as though in a rage of anger and horror. Something flashed from her hand. It slithered through the grass at Dikkon's side and came to a stop. By straining his hand and his fingers, he managed to gather it in—a small hunting knife. It had an edge like fire. It hit instantly through the first cord that it touched, and the bonds loosened all along his right arm.

Sam Prentiss was answering the last appeal. "I've seen you work, Eddie," he replied to the girl. "You've turned better men than him into fools and half-wits, and you've done it with a couple of smiles, eh? You had me in the palm of your hand, once. Listen, Eddie. You had the kid woozy. But he's a fighting fool. I know about him. Still waters . . . and all that kind of stuff."

The arms of Dikkon were free. He touched the ropes that bound his knees and the pressure loosened. He slipped the edge across the tight bonds that held his ankles, and now all constraint was gone from him.

He looked up. The stars were like ten thousand dancing white fires of hope to Dikkon.

"Got the straws fixed?" Tucker asked.

"I got 'em fixed."

Edith broke in again: "Willie, you won't stand for it? Please stick by me, Willie. It's the worst sort of cowardly murder."

"Hold on, Eddie," Tucker said. "I want to stick by you. But after all, as you said yourself a minute ago, business is business. You can't go behind that very well. I'm ready for my draw."

Dikkon busily flexed his hands and worked the muscles of his legs, for he knew he must have the circulation free before he attempted to escape. If he were to bolt for the trees, he would need all his speed.

And then suddenly he knew that he never could reach those trees. Three armed men sat yonder by the fire and, beyond a doubt, every one of them was an expert with guns. They would riddle him with bullets before he had taken ten strides.

"You draw, Jerry."

"This is long enough," Bulger growled.

Now Dikkon fixed a desperate and eager glance on the Colt of Dan Hodge that lay beside the fire. If once he could reach it, no doubt he would be able to shoot his way out of the trouble. And if flight could not save him, what remained for him except to try desperately for the magic of that weapon.

A little silence had fallen on the circle by the fire, and finally Willie Tucker said: "I guess it's you, Bulger."

Bulger started up with an oath.

"Then I'm gonna get it over with," he announced brutally. "Eddie, you get out of here."

She turned her head toward Dikkon; at that very moment he was lurching to his feet.

XI

At the last minute, Jerry Bulger was stopped by an unpleasant thought.

"Hold on," he said. "While I'm away, the three of you'll skin out and take the gun with you."

Prentiss rose and stood beside Bulger.

"You wooden head!" he scoffed. "Go on and do your job. Are you backing out of it?"

"What's that? What's back there?" Bulger called suddenly, and he turned and pointed straight at Dikkon.

He was no longer lashed to the stump of the tree.

If flight was practically impossible, his ghost of a chance lay in reaching the gun that lay there in the charmed circle so near to the fire. And so he bolted for it.

The clever tactician uses subtlety. The blunderer tries to rush a matter through. So it was with Dikkon. He simply stood up and sprinted for the fire.

Bulger and Prentiss, seeing him at the same instant, saw him too late. He was not three paces away. They sprang to the right together. But as it happened, Dikkon had dodged in the same direction. He crashed fairly into them as they both drew their guns. Prentiss received a shoulder in the stomach that doubled him up. Bulger, flung backward, crashed into the fire. The air was filled with shooting clouds of sparks and rang with the wild yell of Bulger, who bounded up again and collided with Willie Tucker, the one cool and efficient man of the trio. They rolled headlong together. Tucker was firing as he fell. Prentiss, in an agony, nevertheless had kept his grip on his gun and was shooting as straight as he could, which was not straight at all.

Through that confusion Dikkon had risen

from the ground where he was flung by the first collision. The revolver of Dan Hodge gleamed within grip of his fingers and immediately before him, or he never would have paused to look for it. As it was, he scooped it up, and leaped into the darkness beyond the fire. Scattered to glowing coals and separate brands, with no flame rising since Bulger fell into it, that fire threw the dimmest of lights, and through the shadows beyond Dikkon ran as a snipe flies, zig-zagging from side to side. Only one shot came near him. It nicked the lobe of his ear and hummed past like a dreadful hornet.

By the edge of the trees, Dikkon saw a long-legged horse starting back in fear, but he caught at the dangling reins. He was dim of eye, so great was his fear. His brain sang and his heart swelled in his breast.

"Come on!" Willie Tucker shouted, running in pursuit.

Dikkon poised the magic gun. Of course it could not miss, but he did not want to take that life unless he had to.

"Come back!" Bulger shouted. "He'll blow you in two!"

The courage of Willie Tucker was depressed. He dropped to the ground and began to fire, but Dikkon had led his horse into the trees. The bullets merely cut with a rattle through the branches or else thudded heavily into the solid trunks, while Dikkon mounted and let the horse drift away of its own accord.

With barriers of pines between, the shouting and the gunshots began to grow fainter at once. It was like turning a corner on a street. Then it died altogether.

He was alone in the night again. The vast trees rose around him. Ten thousand dangers might be lurking in them. One heard of mountain lions that dropped off branches on passers-by, grizzlies rushing out on the unsuspecting wayfarer. And besides, with secret speed the enemy might be slipping up behind him.

Yet Dikkon was not afraid.

He paused and lighted a match. There were six bullets in the old gun. They meant six lives, whether of beast or man, and certainly no danger with more than six heads was apt to rise at him. Dikkon could have sung, so light was his heart.

His odd, cramped life had made him very childish. He hardly knew what barrier was crossed between imagination and the actual world. But it was comfortably proved to his mind that this weapon was a peerless thing. Three men had been willing to take life for the possession of it. Above all, even the girl had been tempted.

The thought of her sobered him a little. He told himself that she was a deceitful little trickster and that she had led him into dreadful danger. But after all, it was her hand which had liberated him again, and no matter how sensible he tried to be, he could not help admitting that, though she had been wonderfully appealing as an apparently innocent girl, she was far more intriguing now. The tame deer is never so beautiful as the wild doe in the forest.

He wanted to head back toward the town but he was utterly lost. Presently the tree trunks began to be more clearly seen. They turned a jet black. The foliage above lightened, and at the top all was a fine silver mist. The moon had risen. He could get out of the woods and climb some height, then, by the moonlight, he might be able to recognize some landmark that would tell him the way home. At any moment he could have left the horse and climbed to the top of a big tree, but Dikkon did not think of that. As a woodsman he was helpless.

Moreover, to tell the truth, the thought of the shoe shop was less and less of an attraction. Only one thing filled him with a sense of guilt and that was the knowledge that he had left the lamp burning in the shop when he started away with the girl. If he could free his conscience of that memory there was nothing to draw him back. The sweetness of the pines filled his lungs, filled his heart. That forest was turned into a fairyland for Dikkon, and if there was danger in it, that was only to be expected in fairylands.

So he went on.

Two or three times he tried to lay out courses, but they led nowhere. At last he allowed the horse to follow its own head. With the reins hanging loosely on its neck, it drifted along as though it understood the way. Now and then it paused, pricking its short ears to listen. Sometimes in those pauses it turned its head and looked back at its rider, so that Dikkon felt a comfortable sense of partnership.

They came to a brook, wide, filled with noise and white water, but the horse went straight into it, as though it had crossed the stream a thousand times before. The water foamed hardly higher than the hocks of the horse, and then they climbed up the farther bank. The forest grew less dense there. There were avenues filled with the silver of the moon, and at last they came out on a clearing.

It was more than a clearing. It was a glacial meadow, with a surface as level as a lawn. The trees stood about it in a lofty, solid ring, and in the center of this spacious meadow there was a house with two stories, a barn and a shed behind it, and several small stacks of hay.

Dikkon suddenly was tired. His head ached with weariness and his eyes were heavy, so he rode straight up to the house, vaguely aware of the sweet scent of drying clover as he passed the nearest stack of hay.

He did not need to knock at the door. The horse

came to a halt and neighed so loudly and strongly that Dikkon was shaken from head to foot. In thunder the piercing echoes came back. Dikkon was frightened by the noise.

At once a window was slammed up.

"Who's there?"

Before Dikkon could answer the speaker went on: "It's you, Mike, ain't it? I'll come down."

The window slammed again, even more loudly than when it had been raised. Steps at once clumped down the stairs, the front door was thrown open and a man in slippers, trousers, and undershirt stepped into the moonlight. It was hard to see his face, for a great brush of hair thrust out above the forehead and left the features in shadow.

"Hey, hello! Who are you?" asked the man of the house. "And where did you get . . ."

He stepped to the head of the horse and fastened his hand on the reins. Dikkon's heart began to race giddily. He forgot the invincible comfort of the revolver.

"I've lost my way," he said. "Can I stay here tonight?"

"You've lost your way, have you?" the other said with much hidden meaning. "Has your horse lost its way? Get down and go on in the house."

Dikkon obeyed. The man led the horse toward the barn.

"Wait at the front door," he called back over his

shoulder, apparently changing his mind after his first invitation.

Dikkon obediently waited at the front door, heartily wishing that he could have found a kinder host, but then he remembered the gun and felt at ease again.

The man of the bushy forelock returned after a few minutes.

"Who are you?" he asked, planting himself in front of the boy.

"I'm Lew Dikkon."

"Lew Dikkon. Never heard that moniker. Mike send you?"

"No."

"Who did?"

Dikkon was silent, because there was no answer to this question.

"Well," snarled the other, "I suppose you don't have to talk. C'mon!"

He led the way into the house. "Close the door after you," he commanded.

Dikkon obeyed and followed up a steep flight of stairs to the upper floor. A long narrow hall led through the house, and Dikkon was shown through a door into a big, bare room. There was one chair, a washstand, and an iron cot.

It was made more desolate by the shining of the moon, which slid through the open window and showed the gaping cracks on the floor. It was a poorly built house. Though there had been little wind outdoors, yet so many drafts whistled and moaned through the place that there seemed a gale blowing.

"Here you are," said the man of the house, and slammed the door heavily.

Then the key turned noisily in the lock.

XII

That noise of the key in the lock snapped back a shutter in the brain of Dikkon. It let in the light and what he saw was danger. But more than danger, two things counted with him just then: he was mightily tired, and the revolver of Dan Hodge, with its five indentations in the handle, was in his possession. He therefore could afford to smile. He was the winner whatever happened, and if trouble came his way, then let luck help at least the first six of the troublemakers.

He wedged a chair under the inner knob of the door. Under the window he placed the washstand. Because it was a creaking, weak-kneed affair, and it threatened to collapse whenever it was stirred, anyone venturing through that window would have to step on that washstand or push it aside, and in either case it would give a warning.

When he had made these preparations, Dikkon remembered that he was very hungry, but the memory was forgotten as soon as he had stretched himself on the bed. He pulled a blanket over him and slept instantly, profoundly, dreamlessly.

He wakened with a mind as clear as a standing pool under a starry sky. Someone was in the room!

He listened again. Someone was in the room, between him and the window. Softly, softly, little by little, he slipped his hand beneath his pillow. He found the revolver and gradually drew it forth. Then his racing heart slowed; his nerves grew steady.

He could remember having lain awake on other windy nights, and heard ghostly footfalls whispering up the halls, and pausing at his door to listen—then the slight creak of the doorknob turning—then the breathing of the danger in his very room.

So he listened now, and across the floor came the unknown through the darkness.

How dark it was! The moon either had set or was behind piled clouds. The window he could distinguish as the faintest of blurs, but straining his eyes against that blur he saw a slight outline. It stirred.

No matter what he had heard and guessed, the actual sight shocked him. He steadied himself. Sudden ferocity poured through the veins of Dikkon and made him set his teeth. He leveled the fatal gun.

The image came straight up to the bed, but so slowly that it barely drifted. A minute hand on a clock would have moved almost as fast.

"Stand," Dikkon snapped, "or . . . I'll blow your head off!"

He had heard that said, or he had read it. It came by instinct to his lips.

Then he heard a hushed, gasping whisper.

"Don't shoot. Don't shoot!"

The form stirred back.

"Stand tight," Dikkon ordered. "Do you think I'm fooling?"

The silhouette no longer moved.

"Throw up your hands!" Dikkon said.

Obediently, the silhouette's arms were extended upward toward the ceiling.

"Good gracious!" said the voice of a girl, "can you see in the dark?"

It was she!

He turned that fact slowly in his numbed brain. Then he slipped from the bed. He found her. He drew down her hands and found them cold and rather tremulous under his touch. He took her to the window. The moon had not set. It was only behind a cloud, and there, at the window, was sufficient light for him to see her face—or rather, to guess at it.

"They were right . . . you are a . . . ," her whisper stopped.

"They sent you up here?" he asked.

She did not answer.

"They sent you here to steal the gun?"

"Yes," she replied.

"How did they know that I'd be in this house?" he asked her.

"I don't know," she replied. "No, they didn't know. Who would have guessed that you'd be such a daredevil and dare to come to their own house?"

Dikkon caught his breath hard. He had walked straight into the den of the lions.

"Only an odd chance brought 'em back here, though," said the girl. "It was only a lucky chance that brought 'em here. They wanted to hunt for you back toward town, but finally they decided that they were fairly beaten. They came home. You are a daredevil, Dikkon."

She said it with complete reverence and awe.

Dikkon began to breathe again, though his brain still was half in darkness.

His silence seemed to frighten her. "What are you going to do with me?" she asked.

"I don't know," said Dikkon. "You took me into the trap."

"I let you out again, though," said the girl.

"Does that square things?"

"No," she answered honestly.

"Will you talk fair and square to me?"

"I will."

"Where are they now?"

"Bulger is in the hall. So is Harry."

"Who is Harry?"

"You know. The man who took you in."

"Well?"

"Prentiss and Tucker are under the window with their rifles."

"And your brother?"

"If he were here, do you think he would have let me come up on this job?"

Dikkon was silent. He felt that he should have known that sort of blood did not flow in the veins of her brother.

"What are you going to do with me?" she asked again.

He had been thinking of that from the first. Immense power lay in his hands, represented by that revolver, the heirloom descended obliquely to him from the dead man.

"I don't know. I don't know," he murmured. "What do you want to do?"

"I'll try to bargain with them. They may let you go free if you'll turn me loose."

"No," he answered almost instantly. "They'll see you dead ten times before they'll give up this gun."

She sighed, and he knew that she admitted the truth of that.

"If I turned you free anyway?"

"Would you dream of doing that?" she asked.

"I'm trying to think."

She waited, silent. In the dim light he saw her hands clasped suddenly together and knew that she was under an intense strain.

"How long have you been with that gang?" he asked her.

"Three months," she said instantly.

"Is that all?"

"All?" she answered. And there was much meaning in that word.

"Why did you join them?"

"I can't tell you."

"You'd better."

"Are you working for the law?" she asked him suddenly.

"No," he replied, honestly enough.

"It's no good asking. I can't tell you."

"If you go back to them, will you stay with them?"

"I . . . I don't know."

"Are you crying?" asked Dikkon.

"I'm t-trying not to," she whispered.

He touched her face. It was cold and wet with tears.

"So!" Dikkon said.

They were not pretended tears. At least, he could be sure of that.

"I'm going to take you away with me," he said.

"How can you do that?"

"There are four of them?"

"Yes."

"I have six lives in my hand," Dikkon said quietly.

He believed what he said, and the firmness of his belief gave a wonderful quality to his voice. He heard a faint gasp in reply.

"Now you follow me," Dikkon said. "Don't be afraid. There are only four of them. I have six good bullets in this gun."

He drew her across the room, holding her by one hand.

Once she drew back a little and he heard her whisper: "Oh, heaven help me."

He pitied her, but there was no time to stop and comfort her. He reached the door of the room.

"Have you the key to this?" he asked her, suddenly remembering that it was closed and locked.

"Yes." She gave it to him.

"You're not going out in the hall?" she pleaded suddenly. "You're not going to do that? They're waiting. They'll shoot to kill."

"Which way are they?"

"Down to the left."

"I don't want to harm them," Dikkon said. "I'll give them a warning."

He unlocked the door and threw it wide,

Down the hall he heard a gasp: "He's coming, Harry. Look sharp!"

Dikkon said loudly: "I know where you are, and I'm coming straight down the hall. If a gun

228

flashes, I'll kill you both, and heaven have mercy on your souls."

Then he stepped out into the hallway, the revolver poised in his hand. He felt merely a vague pity for those two who waited there, nursing their rifles. They, also, knew that immortal power was in his possession.

As he moved through the doorway, the girl threw back her weight with sudden violence, gasping: "No, no!"

"Shoot, Harry!" cried the voice of Bulger. "Give it to him!"

Two rifles crashed. Two long spurts of fire appeared down the hall, and by that light Dikkon saw two men, kneeling, shoulder to shoulder, filling the narrow hall from side to side, the long guns aimed, the tense faces behind them. But both bullets missed his charmed life.

Slowly, pitying them even now, he fired. He heard a distinct spatting sound, as of a fist striking flesh. On its heels a cry rang through the hallway.

He had claimed his first victim with the magic gun!

XIII

The men had been kneeling side by side, their shoulders almost wedged together. Dikkon could not have missed unless he shot over their heads or into the floor. But it did not occur to him that the shot was either difficult or easy; it was inevitable that for every bullet from this famous weapon a man must go down.

He was so confident, so at ease, that he even paused there in the dark of the hallway. The wounded man was trying to stifle groans; they could hear him dragging himself away.

"I'm sorry," said Dikkon to the girl. "I'm sorry that I had to shoot one of them. But you saw that they shot first. They forced me to do it!"

She said nothing at all. Her hand was balled into a tight fist in his grip, and yet she followed without once drawing back.

They heard the stricken voice of Harry whining with pain and terror, a voice kept low, lest it should reach the enemy ears.

"He's killed me, Jerry. Don'cha leave me, kid. Jerry, for Heaven's sake help me out of this. Help me down the stairs. Oh, he's killed me, Jerry!"

It was not the voice of a man in agony from a wound, but rather that of one very sick, very exhausted.

Dikkon said quietly, as he went down the hall: "I won't shoot you again, Harry. Lie still. I'll do you no more harm."

Down the stairs they heard Jerry clumping in wild flight. He crashed against the outer wall at the first landing; the whole house shook.

They went by Harry. He began to mumble. "Do sump'n for me. Pity's sake, boy, you've killed me!"

Dikkon paused.

"We'd better do something for him," he said to the girl. "Will you help me?"

"Yes, yes!" she whispered.

"You won't try to run away if I let you go?"

"I won't. I won't!"

He released her and struck a match.

They saw the white face of Harry beneath them, relaxed in hopelessness. Almost before the first blue flare of the match had turned to yellow flame, Edith was on her knees beside the wounded man. and opening his coat. She had a knife in her hand. Through the shirt and undershirt she slashed rapidly, Dikkon lighting one match after another, while Harry groaned: "Bless you, folks! Bless you! If I live, I'm gonna go straight. I'm gonna find you! I'll be your slave for life, if you save me!"

Dikkon compressed his lips a little and felt dizzy at the sight of the blood. "Am I gonna go, Eddie?" whispered Harry.

"Keep your head up, you poor flannel-mouth!" said the girl cruelly.

"That's a way to talk to maybe a dyin' man!" moaned the victim.

"You've no more backbone than a rabbit," said the girl. "If you give up, you're dead. Put your teeth together and fight it, Harry. Do anything, except soften like a wet sponge!"

She added: "Turn on your left side."

He obeyed with a gasp. His right side was bared now. The girl covered the wounds with the rags she had cut away from his clothing.

Then she turned to Dikkon, saying sharply: "You get out of this. They'll be waiting for you. They'll kill you, Lew Dikkon, as sure as you're a white man!"

"There are only three of them left," said Dikkon simply. "And I still have five shots."

By the light of a dying match, he saw her eyes widen and her lips part.

Then, as the match went out, her crisp voice came through the darkness.

"Go back into your room, then, and get the lamp and light it and bring it here. Hurry!"

He hurried. He was glad to do something to get the faintness out of his brain. He stumbled over a chair in the room, found and lighted the lamp, and brought it back, the flooring of the hall creaking under his stride. He placed the lamp on the floor.

"That's better!" she said. "Are there any sheets in this rat hole, Harry?"

"Not a one in the house, Eddie."

"Well—we'll make out without 'em. Now keep your teeth together and show me you're a man!"

She snapped at Dikkon: "Hold this! Pull here! Harder! That's better—turn him a little—"

A gasping groan forced its way through the teeth of Harry.

She panted, for she was working hard: "Start thanking your luck, Harry! You're only nicked through the ribs. Half an inch farther in, and you'd be a dead man."

"Oh, Eddie, am I gonna live? Am I gonna live?"

"Live? A hundred years!"

He closed his eyes. A long groan came, but it was a groan of utter relief and joy.

With wonderful speed and surety, with far more wonderful strength it seemed to Dikkon, the girl worked. The bandage was made and drawn so tight that it bit into the flesh of Harry.

Suddenly she rocked back on her knees.

"That's about all," she said

"Water, Eddie! Dear old Eddie, gimme a drink of water, and I'll bless you for it."

"Shut up!" said Eddie sharply. "Can we carry him into that room?" she asked Dikkon.

"Yes."

"Now brace yourself, Harry. This will be a strain."

There was a tug and a strain. Dikkon took the man's head and shoulders, and the legs were carried by the girl. Harry, with clenched teeth, endured. They carried him through the first door and laid him out on a bed. There he stretched himself a little and closed his eyes.

"I'm gonna live—water!" he said. The girl disappeared; Dikkon placed the lamp on the table beside the bed. "Turn up the flame," said Harry. "I can stand things better. I wish to goodness that the sun would rise. I'd live, then! You, kid—you're white—you're white—you're white!"

He caught the hand of Dikkon and held it in a pulsing, fluttering grasp. The girl came back with a pitcher of water and a glass. Dikkon raised the head of Harry and she presented the drink. After he had quaffed it, he lay back, breathing very hard, but worshiping the girl with his eyes.

"You ain't a woman, Eddie," said he. "You're an angel. I always said that, you little spitfire."

"Can we leave him now?" asked Dikkon.

"We can. He'll pull through well enough."

"Good-by, kid. Good-by, Eddie. You've hurt me, but I wish you luck!"

They left the room and stood in the dark hall.

"Will you stay here until the morning?" Edith asked humbly.

"I think we'd better go on," said Dikkon. "There are only three of them now, but they might send for help."

234

She gasped.

"You don't *know* what fear is; you don't even guess at it!" said she.

"Ah, but I do! I'm afraid, right enough! But with the gun, you know—we'd better go carefully. They might be sneaking into the house."

She said with ardor: "They'd rather be in a tiger's cage than in this house, Lew Dikkon. Jerry's found them, by this time, and he's told them!"

They went down the hall together.

"I won't have to drag you along?" said Dikkon. "You'll come with me willingly?"

"What do you want to do with me?"

"I don't know. just get you away from these people. That's the first thing, I suppose."

"I'll come, then," she said. "I'll come, if you can do miracles—if you can get us away from this place—but you can't, man! You've done wonderfully. Everyone will admit that. Only, you can't do absolutely impossible things. Nobody can. They'll lie in the brush and shoot you down. The best thing is to split the profits with them!"

He hardly understood the last part of the speech, but he answered savagely, for his blood rose as he thought of what they had done, and more of what they had planned to do: "I'll never speak a word to them, except with a Colt. I'll never give way an inch to them, Eddie—may I call you that?"

"Of course. You're going to make a break for it, then?"

They came to the rear door. Dikkon opened it. The hinges squeaked so loudly that Eddie clutched his arm in fear.

"That gives us away! For Heaven's sake don't venture out!" she said.

He hesitated. The moon was still banked away behind heavy clouds. There was not a star out.

"It isn't a good light for shooting," observed Dikkon.

"Prentiss and Tucker hardly can miss. Look!"

There was a five-gallon tin standing beside the door. She kicked it down the steps. It hardly had reached the ground before rifles began to ring; they heard the clanging of the tin as the bullets whipped cleanly through it. It turned and flopped heavily on another side.

"Light enough! They could kill a regiment by that light," said the girl.

"It looks very bad," admitted Dikkon soberly. "I don't know what to do."

"Wait a moment and listen," said the girl. "It's my brother coming! He's coming!"

Through the dark, they heard the beat of hoofs, now muffled on pine needles, now falling with a clang on rock. It was a noise drawing rapidly toward the house out of the woods.

XIV

Dikkon hardly knew whether to welcome the thought of the girl's brother or not. He might throw in with the rest of the thugs. And the loud cry of Prentiss at that moment re-enforced the idea.

"Is that you? Hey, Mike, is that you?"

"Here!" called someone in the distance.

There was a shout from the three in the brush near the house. Horses broke from the woods, and clearly, above the brush, Dikkon saw five riders sweep across the meadow toward the shrubbery. They came in among it, crashing.

"Where's Prentiss?"

"Here! Here! I'm glad to see you! That fool of a kid has come out and got the gun away from us!"

Dikkon turned to the girl.

"I can't ask you to go with me now," he said. "It's going to be a narrow pinch. There are eight of them! Good-by, Eddie. I'm going to make a break for it."

"Wait, wait!" she urged, clinging to him. "There's something wrong, out there!"

"Where's Bulger and Tucker?" called a voice from the horsemen, and the voice was rather familiar to Dikkon.

"Here!"

"Then throw up your hands, you cutthroats!" called he who now was unmistakably Steve Martin. "Stick up your hands and do it pronto! I want the three of you, and I want you bad! Surround 'em, boys. If they so much as wink, shoot 'em full of holes!"

"You see!" breathed Eddie.

Dikkon gaped. He was totally unprepared for such a sudden and happy outcome.

Protests poured freely from the lips of the three criminals. Steve Martin began to exult aloud.

"What were you doing out here? Shooting off guns to show me the way to your house? Or were you just out having a little practice in the dark of the moon?"

He began to laugh. Jerry Bulger broke in with a violent stream of abuse.

"What you want with me? What you got on me?" he asked. "It ain't a crime to fire off a gun by night. I ain't disturbin' the peace, away out here!"

"Sure you ain't," said Steve Martin. "It ain't for disturbing of the peace that I want you. It's something a mite worse. I want the three of you for the murder of Dan Hodge!"

The words rang in the heart of Dikkon like a bell. The murder of Dan Hodge! Prentiss, he could guess, would wince when he heard that accusation. "They did it!" murmured Dikkon.

"The cowards! The sneaks and murderers!" whispered the girl in detestation. "Of course they did it! And my poor old Mike herding with low rascals like those!"

She added: "But Mike didn't have any hand in it. I'm sure of that. I'll really swear that!"

"Of course he had no hand in it. Listen!"

Tucker was raging: "I never seen Dan Hodge in my life," he vowed. "I'm gonna be even with you for this here, Martin!"

"Oh, shut your mouth," snarled Martin angrily. "You never seen Hodge in your life! No, nor in his. But you seen him dying or dead, right enough. Or else, you seen his stuff!"

"What stuff?"

"Look here, boys, you might as well stop throwing the bluff, because it don't buy you nothin' with me. Will you cut it? The guy blew on you all."

"What *guy?*" asked the sharp voice of Prentiss.

And Dikkon thought that there was a ring of apprehension in the tone.

"*The* guy, my son. What one d'you think? Nobody but old Izzie Bernstein himself!" retorted Martin.

He reduced them to silence with this, and then he could be heard saying: "Tie them, and tie them so tight that their wrists'll ache. These three boys will try to break if they can. I'm gonna hang the three of you for that murder. I don't mind tellin'

239

you that. I'm gonna hang all three of you, you dogs!"

"What's the fellow got on me? Nothin'!" declared Jerry Bulger, without conviction.

"He's got plenty on all three of you," declared Martin. "No sooner put pressure on him than he ran words faster than a cider press runs apple juice. He's a yellow dog."

"He is!" vowed Prentiss.

"But he got you all cold. He had the facts and the dates. We even got some letters out of him. And what's more, we know why you wanted to kill Hodge."

"Let the judge say the rest, will you?" snarled Prentiss.

"I'll do my own talking. Because I want to tell you that the boy who puts the stuff in my hands may go a lot easier than the rest. The boy that'll place the thing in my hands and help the State with a little evidence—well, we'll fix him up. Now who's it gonna be?"

"I'll see you farther, first," said Prentiss. "Besides, since you know so much," he added, with growing venom, "I ain't got it. Not Bulger, nor none of us."

"Because you buried it, I suppose?" asked Martin.

"We never had our hands on it," said Prentiss. "But I'll tell you who has! It's the kid that you let grow up under your nose in town—a murderin' thief and sneak and general bad one. Him—he's got it—and he's got it in the house there yonder with him!"

The hands of the girl closed on the arm of Dikkon.

"The coward!" she was whispering through her teeth. "The coward, the coward! I told Mike what sort of a cur he was. I wish he was here to listen to that!"

Then she added: "They're going to come for you. What to do?"

"I don't know," said Dikkon gravely.

"They want it," said the girl. "Give it up to them! Give it up to them! After all, is it worth such a fight?"

"Give it up?" echoed Dikkon vaguely. "Give it up? I'd rather give up my life!"

Her hands fell from his arm.

"Very well," said she. "If you want it that badly, you'll keep it—and the bullets it brings your way. I'm sorry, Dikkon. I thought you cut above that sort of thing!"

He wondered at what she said, and it brought a frown on his forehead. In some manner he had disgusted her, it appeared. Though why it should seem strange that a man would want to fight for such a famous weapon was beyond him! However, he felt that her ways of thought must follow dim and delicate trails where he could not pass.

"Good-by!" said Dikkon. "Since the law has come, I'll leave you here. You'll be safe with them."

"What are you going to do?"

"Go to the barn, get a horse, and ride away."

"They'll be sure to see you."

"They're talking a great deal," answered Dikkon obliquely.

But he had in mind a maxim of his stern uncle: "Him that talks can't set to work!"

By this he had justified the dreary hours of silence upon their workbench.

And in fact, an argument was raging between Martin and the three he had captured. They insisted that the spoils of Dan Hodge were in the possession of Dikkon in the house; the sheriff laughed at their bluff.

Dikkon walked quietly down the back steps of the house and started across the opening for the barn. He wanted to sprint with all his might, but remembered a lesson early learned—that the swiftly moving thing is most readily seen.

So he sauntered, picking his steps with the greatest care to avoid stepping on a twig. He crossed the halfway point. He neared the mouth of the yawning barn door, and then a shrill voice cut the air: "There he goes now! There! By the barn door!"

Dikkon covered the remaining distance with a bound. He entered the warm, hay-scented darkness; he heard the sound of an animal crunching hay. But next to the door he made out the glimmer of a gray horse. On the wall just behind it hung a saddle.

A slender form darted past him.

"Back the horse out!" cried the girl's voice softly. "Not the gray—not the gray, stupid! The next one! Quick! Quick!"

Before he had the head rope untied from the stall, she had dragged a saddle on the back of the horse. She thrust the end of the girth into his hand and, while he worked at cinching up, she jerked the bridle on the animal's head.

"There's a back way. Come fast!"

She fled before him. He followed, stumbling, slipping, terribly frightened. It was one thing to stand opposed to guilty men, desperate and grim criminals—but the law was different. He hardly knew how it was that the law stood against him, but he knew that he would die sooner than give up the gun.

Horses rushed up to the front of the barn. Dikkon heard the sound of many voices.

"Get a light here!"

"No time for that! Push in with me, Joe! We'll nail him!"

That was Steve Martin speaking.

Then, from the distance, a shrill command: "Hey, Martin, cut in around the barn. He'll get out the back way! He'll skin out the back way!"

243

"Here we are!" cried Eddie.

She thrust open a narrow door. The damp night air was in Dikkon's face.

"Heaven bless you!" said Dikkon, standing under the rolling clouds.

"Go quick! D'you hear?" she urged.

Hoofbeats were sweeping around the side of the barn. He looked to the dark trees that rose just before him. He thought of the rushing peril. Still he could not go. Then he knew the thing which remained to do. He took her firmly in his arms, and kissed her.

"You blessed—idiot!" said the girl.

But Dikkon was in the saddle, and plunging for the woods.

XV

They came behind him with horses that groaned with speed, and with flashing guns. The bullets crashed before him through the woods, and twice he turned with poised gun, and twice he could not fire. For, after all, these were the arms of the law, and he had no right to defend himself. Bitterly he gritted his teeth. It was the mystery of the thing that baffled him. Why should they ride so furiously after him for the sake of a gun which he had bought with his own money, hard-earned?

But if he could not rely upon his gun, he could rely upon the horse which the girl had chosen for him. It was delicate on the rein, but strong and speedy. Swerving through the trees, half a dozen times it nearly twisted Dikkon from the saddle, but also it left the pursuit far behind.

He came out in the open country beyond. He could not turn back toward the town. Before him arose ragged heights, and toward these he pressed forward. There was only an occasional rattling of hoofs behind him. Presently he was riding through the night accompanied only by the noise which his own mount made upon the rocks and the gravel.

When Dikkon was sure of his momentary security, he brought his horse to a walk and surrendered himself to despair. He had read something of outlaws; he had read and heard much of their lives and their endings. Always it was a bullet or a rope that finished them, and their careers were short. Sometimes a dexterous villain endured for a few years by means of murders, craft, treachery, guile. But Dikkon knew that in himself there were none of these qualities.

With that magic gun which he held in his hand, he would have gone careering through the world righting wrong and succoring the distressed like a knight of the ancient days, but this rightful exercise of his power was stolen from him. He must live like a lost wolf.

So he drove himself on into the upper recesses of the mountains and determined that he would not flinch. He would do as the girl had advised poor Harry to do—set his teeth and endure!

For three days, therefore, he endured. He grew thin. His back ached with famine like a starved wolf's. And at last he determined that he must go down among men in order to satisfy his hunger. Certainly he could not subsist, like a squirrel, on pine nuts.

He began to move at the setting of the sun; he was in the lower valley in the red of the evening; he was at the side of a ranch house by dark, and under him his horse was as full of fettle as when he had sat on its back for the first moment. It was like silk—as smooth and as strong. And he never galloped it into the wind of its own speed without thinking of the girl who had given him such a mount. For she, like it, was nervous, keen, and strong as fine steel. He was filled with wonder and with fear as he thought of her. He could not tell whether he most loved or dreaded the thought of her.

He went to a barn behind the ranch house, first. There he pilfered a fork of hay. He found the grain box, and making a depression in the top of the hay, he poured a hatful of grain into it. His horse was provided for. He himself was so hungry that he was half inclined to begin a meal on the sweet-smelling crushed barley.

Then he slipped back to the house and skirted it softly. People were in the dining room around a long table. In the kitchen a cook was busily at work.

If he went in to buy a meal, he would be seated at the table with the other people—the long double row of cowpunchers who bent low over their food. However, food he must have. And he could not steal it like a guilty rascal!

Dikkon went to the kitchen door. The cook howled an order to enter over his shoulder, and Dikkon came in. Food? Of course! The boss of that job never sent men away hungry. Go in and sit down. There were two or three extra places at the foot of the table.

Dikkon went in, slowly. He was prepared to have a battery of eyes turned upon him. Instead, he got for a greeting only a mumble from the full mouths of the half dozen nearest his end of the table. He sat down under the blaze of the gasoline lamp, and hoped that, before trouble started, he might at least taste food and be relieved of the troublesome singing in his ears.

Great dishes, nearly emptied, were passed down to him in a volley. He helped himself and then, as he began to eat, he forgot all peril, all strangeness. It was the most perfect moment of his life.

He admitted that to himself with a sort of sad wonder. There was the girl. What of her? But no matter what she meant to him, there never had been a moment when she had stirred him as he was stirred now. He ate, and the doors of happiness opened before him.

The others were finishing their second cups of coffee as he swiftly devoured a second plateful. They began to tip back their chairs; clouds of blue-brown tobacco smoke were blown upward from strong lungs; talk began to boom and rumble. About a bogged-down cow in a "tank"; about the pitching of the new roan colt.

"They haven't seen Dikkon for three days."

That out of a clear sky. He bowed his face over his coffee cup and hoped that the tremor of his hands had not been seen.

"They won't see him no more. He's gone."

"He never looked like a gunfighter."

"He never did."

Two of them, apparently, remembered him! He ventured a glance at them and knew them well enough. Thank goodness his face was thinner and coated with brown, with a nose crimsoned by the weather. That might disguise him well enough.

"He looked like kind of a half-wit, to me."

"Dumb he sure looked. He must've been a deep one."

"Riding back to their own house to put up! That was nerve."

"Oh, nothing but. Well, he's got his fortune."

"How much is it worth?"

"Fifty thousand, they say."

"For one diamond?"

"Sure."

"An awful lot for one stone, ain't it?"

"You dunno nothin', Pete. You got no eddication. Say, kid, they can sell one diamond for millions, I guess."

A diamond!

Dikkon concealed his face behind his raised coffee cup. Diamond! That tallied with certain expressions which had puzzled him in the past. But what had a diamond to do with Dan Hodge's old gun?

"But what had the fool girl got to do with it? What did old man Murray's girl have to mix up in the thing for. It wasn't hers, was it?"

"It was her brother that started the thing."

"He's a crazy kid. I know Mike Murray. Redhead is always kind of nutty. That's for you, Bill! I didn't know he was mixed in."

"You ain't heard all the news, then! Hodge swiped that diamond from Mrs. Childers."

"I knew that."

"Well, young Murray was crazy about Mrs. Childers's girl."

"Everybody knows that."

"Shut up. Or else, you tell it."

"Go on."

"Mrs. Childers got sick and went to bed, she

was so worried about that dog-gone diamond."

"Fifty thousand is worth getting sick over."

"Her daughter passes on the worry to 'Red' Murray. 'I'll get the diamond back,' says Mike.

"Well, they sort of expected that he'd have to live up to his promise. What did he do? Got professionals. He done something himself, first of all. Found out that Dan Hodge was likely the man that had the diamond. Then he got the professors."

"What do you mean?"

"What's Bulger and Prentiss and the rest?"

"I know. Old-time crooks."

"Sure, professionals. Mike Murray says to them: 'I'll put you on the trail of a job. I'll pay you handsome. You deliver the goods to me.' They began to track Hodge. They find that Bernstein, the fence, is staying in town. Well, Hodge will come in to him some Saturday, after work is over in the evening. That straight?"

"Sure, that's sense."

"Well, he come in. They took a short cut. Didn't talk, just murdered him. Searched him, didn't find what they wanted. Martin got there too quick for them. Then they got a tip from the fence that Hodge had the diamond in an old gun with five notches in it. And then they—"

Dikkon's head swam. But he steadied himself again. He could not afford to miss what was said.

"They tried to buy the gun at the auction the next day. But after they'd run up the price a ways, this kid, Dikkon, he begun to bid. Prentiss seen that the kid wanted the gun. He didn't want to bid against him. Might make other folks too curious. Just thought that he'd take the gun away from him afterward. Tried that and got nothing. Neither did Bulger.

"Then they rung in Red Mike Murray's sister. They told her what was wrong. If she could get Dikkon out in the woods, they'd handle him right enough. They'd get the diamond. They wouldn't hurt him none. She tried to get Mike's advice. Mike was away somewheres. All she knew was that he'd trusted these gents, and she was too young, mebbe, not to trust them, too. You see, the whole gang of 'em once had worked for years on the old Murray place. They'd seen her grown up. They called her by a nickname. Y'understand? She didn't really think they could be bad uns, even if the sheriff did want them. So she sashays into town and trails young Dikkon out along with her into the woods. Game was all that she was, the little fool!"

"Fool is right!"

"But when those hounds got their hands on the gun with the diamond in it, they forgot that they was hired. They wanted the loot, as Mike should've known that they would. They begin to wrangle—the kid busts loose and gets the gun

251

away again. And there you are. You all know the rest of it. The sheriff got this out of Bernstein, and Red Murray, and his sister."

"This Dikkon," said Pete, "if he is—"

His voice ended. Dikkon looked up sharply and saw that Pete, with startled, wide eyes, was staring straight at him, and seeing him for the first time, and recognizing him at last.

XVI

He could not move, at first. The glory of his world had crashed down about his ears. He, the brave knight, had been nothing but a poor shoemaker carrying through wild adventures a rattling, useless old gun, valuable only because it had been used as a trick hiding place.

He saw that, and suddenly Dikkon was so filled with a sense of the irony of this thing, and with a sort of despair, that he stood up and stared calmly up and down the table.

No man moved for a gun. No man could move his riveted eyes. Only there was a faint whisper:

"It's Dikkon!"

Of course it was Dikkon, and they were enchanted and turned to stone by a false magic. He had ceased to believe in his weapon, or himself; but their belief was how mightily potent! Twelve strong men—twelve good men and true, and they dared not move. Dikkon smiled a little. Those who watched thought it was a smile of superior contempt. He turned on his heel and walked slowly from the room. In the kitchen, he heard a sudden clamor break out behind him. But the clamor was stilled at once.

"You boys keep still. This ain't our fight. Let him go. You'll spend more blood than you'll get glory if you go after that gent!"

And no one moved to pursue him!

He went back to his horse, mounted it, and rode away into the valley, letting the horse drift on the home track. Now that he knew what to look for, the thing was absurdly simple. He only had to light two matches before he found the catch, and one side of the handle of the gun stirred back, then fell away into his hand, and with it a flashing lump of ice, blue-white, filled with fires. He held it in the cup of his hand and examined it again more carefully.

Why had they not gone to the sheriff and made their complaint to him, when they knew that Dikkon had the weapon and the treasure in it? Because, no doubt, they thought that he would have concealed the gun the instant the sheriff showed his face in the door of the shop. Because, too, the three criminals were simply working to get the jewel into their own hands, not to restore it to its rightful master.

He could see the thing easily enough, now. But

here it was all to end—his own greatness, and the greatness of the magic gun!

All that night he drifted on toward the town and there he arrived when the sun was barely up, but the place already was beginning to live. He went straight to the house of Steve Martin and rapped at the door. Martin, himself, opened the door. He started back at the sudden vision of Dikkon.

"It's all right," said Dikkon. "I've not come to make any trouble. Here's the diamond!"

He put the flaming beauty in the sheriff's hand.

"Now jail, I suppose?" said Dikkon wearily.

"Jail?" echoed the deputy, open-mouthed. "I dunno for what!"

Dikkon turned from the door. He had left his guilt behind him; he had left the romance of his life, also. So he went back to the shop of his uncle and leaned in the door.

"You're done raisin' trouble, are you?" snapped that old man without a sign of surprise. "Come in here and get to work on that pair of boots for Jarrow. He was in here askin' yesterday. Everything's behindhand. You're gonna have to work every night till mornin'."

Dikkon made no answer. He went back to the bench, and thereafter his uncle referred to the matter only once more, and then with a grunt.

"Hero? Hero? Well!" he growled sarcastically.

And Dikkon felt that the matter was disposed of.

The interest of the townsmen, however, had not fallen away. They began to come in a crowd. They hung in the doorway. They blundered into the shop. They asked foolish questions. They grinned on Dikkon with admiration.

He stood it until noon and then leaped from the bench and confronted them.

"You grinning apes, scatter!" he commanded. "If another of you comes here that ain't got business in the shop . . ."

He had no time to voice his definite threat. They melted away suddenly before him. They even ran from the door. He turned back slowly toward the bench. There was such a red mist before his eyes that he hardly could find his place. There he sat with idle hands, wondering. A week before, could he have acted like that? Would a crowd have fled at his empty voice?

Something had happened. Something had changed!

He resumed his work, however, slowly, dreamily. And between his eyes and the awl a vision kept drifting. He forgot time. Presently a hand touched his shoulder.

"Maybe you'd better come to supper? I got it cooked."

He looked up vaguely, and his uncle backed away with a pathetically frightened, baffled smile, and disappeared through the inner door. Dikkon fell into another dream.

The soft chiming of the clock roused him. It had struck eight, and into the doorway turned a brisk step. He looked up, steeling himself to meet the eyes of Prentiss; but it was only a handsome, red-headed youth, dressed just a shade too well to be a common cowpuncher. A brown, ruddy, cheerful youth. He leaned on the counter.

"You know me?"

"I don't."

"I'm Red Murray."

Dikkon stood up. His hand was grasped. The smile of Red Murray went through him like an electric shock, and all his dreams were twitched away and left him confronting reality again.

"You've kept me from being a fool, Dikkon— the world's grandest fool. You've kept Eddie— who knows from what! I've come for a talk with you. Will you talk?"

"About what?" said Dikkon.

"I hardly know. But when I heard that you were back in here on the workbench, I had to come. I only want to ask you this: D'you like this work? D'you choose it, I mean?"

He indicated the battered, cluttered shop.

"No," said Dikkon, "I don't suppose that I do."

"Ah, then," cried Red Murray, "then you'll let me suggest—"

"What?" said Dikkon.

"I—look here, I can't talk up the idea. But will

you come outside with me? I've got a friend that can put it a lot better!"

Dikkon followed him, wondering. And at the door, he looked out on the heads of two thoroughbreds, delicately made, large and bright of eye, and the small form of a girl standing between them, holding the reins.

The very knees of Dikkon grew weak. He looked up to the skies and there he saw the bright glory of the night. He dropped a hand into his pocket, instinctively, and there his fingers closed over the handle of the Colt.

And before ever she spoke to him; before he had made a step closer to her, Dikkon knew that after all there had been magic mingled in his life, and that the magic and the girl were to stay with him forever.

Additional Copyright Information

About the Author

Max Brand is the best-known pen name of Frederick Faust, creator of Dr. Kildare, Destry, and many other fictional characters popular with readers and viewers worldwide. Faust wrote for a variety of audiences in many genres. His enormous output, totaling approximately thirty million words or the equivalent of five hundred thirty ordinary books, covered nearly every field: crime, fantasy, historical romance, espionage, Westerns, science fiction, adventure, animal stories, love, war, and fashionable society, big business and big medicine. Eighty motion pictures have been based on his works along with many radio and television programs. For good measure, he also published four volumes of poetry. Perhaps no other author has reached more people in such a variety of different ways.

Born in Seattle in 1892, orphaned early, Faust grew up in the rural San Joaquin Valley of California. At Berkeley he became a student rebel and one-man literary movement, contributing prodigiously to all campus publications. Denied a degree because of unconventional conduct, he embarked on a series of adventures culminating in New York City where, after a period of near starvation, he received simultaneous recognition as a serious poet and successful author of fiction. Later, he traveled widely, making his home in New York, then in Florence, Italy, and finally in Los Angeles.

Once the United States entered the Second World War, Faust abandoned his lucrative writing career and his work as a screenwriter to serve as a war correspondent with the infantry in Italy, despite his fifty-one years and a bad heart. He was killed during a night attack on a hilltop village held by the German army. New books based on magazine serials or unpublished manuscripts or restored versions continue to appear so that, alive or dead, he has averaged a new book every six months for seventy-five years. Beyond this, some work by him is newly reprinted every week of every year in one or another format somewhere in the world. A great deal more about this author and his work can be found in *The Max Brand Companion* (Greenwood Press, 1997) edited by Jon Tuska and Vicki Piekarski. His Website is www.MaxBrandOnline.com.

Center Point Large Print
600 Brooks Road / PO Box 1
Thorndike, ME 04986-0001 USA

(207) 568-3717

US & Canada:
1 800 929-9108
www.centerpointlargeprint.com